Flames engulfed the stern

The *Fancy Free*'s forward motion stopped.

"They've hit the engines!" Sir Abner yelled.

George crawled toward the stern to examine the damage. He made a quick about-face as black, oily smoke billowed upward from the bowels of the ship. "The fuel tanks are burning, Dan! We're on fire!"

The pirate vessel, hidden in the thick, rolling smoke, moved in for the final killing run.

Dan Track, his eyes watering and his throat burning, was forced to let go of the submachine gun as the first rounds of a fresh fusillade slammed into the *Fancy Free*.

"Goddamn," he said. "I think we've had it."

Now available in the exciting new series
from Gold Eagle Books

TRACK

TRACK
Drug Runner

PATRICK ANDREWS

A GOLD EAGLE BOOK FROM
W☉RLDWIDE

TORONTO · NEW YORK · LONDON · PARIS
AMSTERDAM · STOCKHOLM · HAMBURG
ATHENS · MILAN · TOKYO · SYDNEY

To My Old Outfit
THE 12TH SPECIAL FORCES GROUP (AIRBORNE)
De Oppresso Liber

First edition April 1986

ISBN 0-373-62012-8

Printed in Canada.

Prologue

It was the end of a glorious day.

The boat bobbed gently in the docile swells eased into a lagoon of the Caribbean Sea. The moon of the new evening, low and bright in the sky, floated a reflected orb of luminous gold on the water. A balmy breeze momentarily fluttered the furled sails and wafted away much of the day's heat.

The boat was a beauty to behold. Teak overlay decks glowed in contrast to a brilliant white hull with deep red striping. The vessel's name and home port were brightly displayed on the stern in handsome script:

Escape to Paradise
Stamford

The people aboard the *Escape* were spending their vacation sailing among the islands south of Hispaniola. Although uninhabited, these small isles had much to offer: the excitement of going ashore to explore or the relaxing isolation of sheltered lagoons such as the one the boat had moored in for the night.

The craft's occupants, two married couples from Connecticut, were treating themselves to a respite from the chilling grasp of New England's harsh winter. For the men, this holiday was a temporary escape from the pressures of middle-management jobs in a large investment firm on Wall Street.

The snorkeling and rigors of sailing had trimmed the guys' waists a bit. The women, happily acquiring magnificent tans to make their friends envious back home, were already in shape from hours of aerobics and indoor jogging at the local health club. They were going into middle age, but they were determined to do it looking good. Both were proud of their figures and wore skimpy bikinis, often tossing the halters aside, something they would never have done within the strict confines of the local yacht club. The husbands acted nonchalant as they stole glances at the boobs of the other man's wife.

Cold beer and barbecued steaks were on the menu for that evening, but clouds of insects swarming out of the island's vegetation had driven the couples below decks to enjoy the repast. A battery-powered stereo blared twenty-year-old songs, the requiem for a youth lost to all but memory.

The loud music covered the sound of the approaching launch.

The men in this small craft were most definitely not on a middle-class, midlife vacation. They were hard-asses, sporting tattoos of various Latin American gangs and scars that announced their allegiance to violence. A rather impressive array of weaponry was also shared among them. Rather than the cheap pistols and switchblades that might be expected among street toughs, their arsenal was modern, expensive and state of the art.

The boat eased alongside, and three of the four men quietly slipped aboard the *Escape*, hardly causing a wobble. One man, obviously the leader, led the way to the companionway. Patient and in no hurry, he devoted almost a quarter of an hour to listening to the sounds below deck to accurately determine how many people were aboard.

Then, signaling with a nod of his head, he led his men below.

The fatter of the two men spotted the intruders first. Shocked into silence, he started to stand up and point as the sudden burst from a Browning Hi-Power pistol clouded his uncomprehending features with blood.

His friend managed to bellow, "Oh, shit!" before he, too, was hit. A bullet punched into his ear and knocked him sprawling into the narrow space between the table and a bunk.

The women instinctively covered their bare breasts, their eyes were wide with horror. Somewhere, behind the panic and terror in their minds, was the image of humiliation and abuse to be suffered at the hands of the thugs who crowded into the cabin.

The intruders had access to more women than they could use. The sight of these half-naked women stirred no lust. As far as the killers were concerned, the women were only a temporary inconvenience that had to be disposed of.

Three pistols barked and kicked, their spiraling slugs slapping into bare flesh and dumping the victims in a heap on top of their husbands. The men hurriedly dragged the bodies up on deck and flung them into the lagoon.

The pirates were experienced and well drilled in this sort of work. They swiftly went about preparing the craft for immediate departure onto the open sea. Meanwhile, the leader went below again to assess the interior of the boat. There was inlaid teak and mahogany in the paneling and cabinet work. He nodded in approval. Once that stuff was torn out, this particular craft could haul at least six tons of marijuana.

The engine was started, and the boat moved slowly out of the lagoon, headed for the open sea.

1

Stubby Boudreaux sat on the dock at his marina and watched with sleepy interest as the Gulfstar Motor Yacht came in out of the open Atlantic and passed the breakwater extending three hundred yards out into the blue water. The craft throttled down to approach the docks.

Stubby, a three-day growth of beard on his fat jowls, expertly spat a stream of tobacco juice between the railings on the dock. "That's some kinda boat," he said to himself. He was comfortably tipped back in an old wooden chair that rested against his weather-beaten plank building, where he operated a combination general store and chandlery.

As owner and operator of the grandly named Stubby's Marina of Key Largo, he sold overpriced fuel, questionable provisions and valuable information on the best fishing of the season, not only in the waters around the Florida Keys where he lived, but also at points farther south in the Caribbean.

Stubby scowled and looked over at the overly large young man in bib overalls who stood at the edge of the dock indolently trailing a fishing line in the water. The marina operator shifted the chaw in his mouth. "Hey, shithead."

The large kid, who appeared to be in his early twenties, continued to fish.

"Hey, shithead!"

No response.

"Hey, shithead!"

The young man slowly turned around. "You call me, Uncle Stubby?"

"O'course I called you! Looky yonder at that boat comin' in."

The heavily muscled youth did as he was told. "Oh, yeah. It's a perty'un, ain't it?"

"Goddamn it, Marvin Leroy! I din't yell at you to just look at the sumbitch. Go over thar and direct him to slip three."

Marvin Leroy Firpo slowly laid his fishing pole down. "Sure thing, Uncle Stubby."

"And help the feller tie up." Stubby, as fat and short as his nickname indicated, shook his head as Marvin Leroy ambled over to tend to the task. "Damn! That boy's got some to go afore he'd be as smart as a Okefenokee mud turtle."

Marvin Leroy ambled down to the slips and waved to the man on the deck. "Tell your pilot to bring her here into number three. Go ahead and throw me yore line, mister. I'll secure the bow."

"Thanks a lot," George Beegh said. He tossed the rope over, then trotted to the stern to tie on there himself.

Up in the flying bridge, Dan Track reversed the starboard screw for a couple of thrusts and brought the boat into the dock. Then he cut the engine. He waved down at Marvin Leroy. "How're you doing?"

"Just fine, thank you kindly," Marvin Leroy said with a friendly, toothy grin. "What can we do fer you folks?"

"We need some fuel, something to eat and some information," Track said. "Think you can help us?"

"I can he'p you with the gas and the vittles, but you'll have to ask my Uncle Stubby fer any information you need. Tha's his department." Marvin guffawed. "He does that and chews on my ass a lot."

Track grinned. "Okay. What's your name?"

"Marvin Leroy Firpo," he replied. "Y'all staying awhile?"

"At least overnight," Track said. "We're pretty tired. We came all the way down here from Stamford, Connecticut."

"Hot damn!" Marvin Leroy said. Then he frowned. "Is that a long ways?"

"Sure is," Track said.

George Beegh hopped from the deck onto the dock. He took a close look at Marvin Leroy, noting his youthfulness and size. "You aren't still growing, are you?"

The big kid grinned. "Well, I'm twenty, and Mama says I got some to go to catch up with my daddy."

"Your daddy's pretty big, is he?" George inquired.

"He was big—he's dead."

"Sorry to hear that," George said.

"Yeah. My Uncle Stubby killed him."

Track leaned over the side. "Yeah?"

"Sure did," Marvin Leroy said. "Daddy was a-beatin' the shit outta Mama—she's Uncle Stubby's sister—and Uncle Stubby came over when he heard her yellin' and carryin' on. He'd tole Daddy not to do that no more, so he hauled off and shot him deader'n hell."

"Damn!" George said. "He just shot him?"

"Uncle Stubby's such a little bitty feller that he'd never o' been able to whup Daddy," Marvin Leroy said. He turned to point at his uncle, but noticed him approaching. "Here he comes now."

Stubby Boudreaux, his belly wobbling like a beach ball in his dirty khakis, walked up and took a look at the stern. He noted the name and glanced up at the man on the flying bridge. "Ahoy, *Fancy Free*."

"How're you doing?" Track said with a wave.

"You the skipper?" Stubby asked.

"Nope," Track answered. "I'm just a guest. My uncle owns her. He and the captain are below."

Stubby wasn't surprised the captain wasn't at the helm. Most of the monied people that owned or were passengers aboard boats preferred to handle them personally, using the captain only when real seamanship was necessary. "I'm the owner and operator of this here marina—Stubby Boudreaux at your service. I heard you tell Marvin Leroy you was gonna stay the night," Stubby said. "I'll need the skipper or the registered owner to sign in. State law, y'know."

"Sure, I'll see to it," Track said. "In the meantime we need fuel and some provisions."

"Where y'all goin'?" Stubby asked.

"That depends on you," Track answered. "Some of our friends told us you're the man down here in Florida with all the information."

Stubby laughed. "They're right, if you don't mind me sayin' so. C'mon up to the store there when you've a mind. We'll take care of your vittles and the information both." He kicked Marvin Leroy. "Gas 'em up, shithead!"

"Yes, sir, Uncle Stubby."

Stubby smiled up at Track. "See y'all directly."

"You bet," Track said. He watched Stubby waddle back to the store on the dock, then turned his attention back to Marvin Leroy. "She's all yours, pal."

"I'll top you off right away," the big youth said, ambling happily over to the fuel pump.

A large black man appeared on deck, followed by a dignified gentleman in his sixties who gave the impression of being very fit despite his age. A young woman, beautiful and well-proportioned, with a thick mane of flowing black hair, appeared behind the two men.

"You or Zulu have to register us for the night," Track said.

Sir Abner Chesterton looked over at Zulu. "Would you be so kind?"

"Of course," Zulu said in a deep, cultured voice. "Part of my duties as sea captain, hey?" He chuckled.

"There's a store over there," Desiree Goth said. "Is that the place we're looking for?"

"Right," Track answered. "Boudreaux's Marina."

The woman walked to the edge of the deck and dropped lightly to the dock. "Let's not waste time."

"After you," Track said. The men joined her, and all five of them trod down the wood walkway to the store.

"By God, they's a passel o' you aboard there!" Stubby marveled as the group entered his small store.

"Sure is," Track said. He offered his hand. "My name's Hunter." He motioned Desiree Goth forward. "This is my wife."

Stubby took in Desiree's aristocratic beauty methodically, from crown to ankle. "How do, ma'am," he said politely. Then he added, "You're French, ain'cha?"

"There is French in my family," Desiree answered in her unidentifiable accent. "But how could you tell?"

"I, too, am of the French persuasion, ma'am," Stubby said. "I'm a misplaced Cajun. My gran'pappy hightailed it—er, that is, he moved from Louisiana to Florida when he was a young man."

"This is my uncle, Mr. Chesterton," Track said.

"How do you do," Sir Abner said.

"And last, but certainly not least—our crew," Track said. "First the captain."

Zulu stepped forward. "I am Captain Baharia," he said, using his cover name. "And this is the mate, Mr. Big."

George Beegh nodded.

"Y'all are quite a group," Stubby said. Marvin Leroy joined them. He stood in the doorway with his hands jammed deep in his overall pockets, grinning in a silly but friendly manner.

Stubby glared at him. "Did you gas 'em up like I said?"

"Yes, sir, Uncle Stubby."

"Tha's good," Stubby said. He turned back to his customers, all smiles. "Now afore we gets to the stores you want to buy, let's talk about where you're wantin' to go."

"We don't know exactly," Track said. "We had some friends sail down here before us. In fact, they mentioned stopping by here in a letter. We were going to meet them, but we haven't heard a word in weeks now. We were hoping you might know where they went."

Stubby frowned thoughtfully. "So they docked here, hey?"

"Yeah. They mentioned your marina in the letter, Monsieur Boudreaux," Desiree said. "They were two couples—the Monroes and the Hamiltons."

"What was the name o' their boat?"

"The *Escape to Paradise*—out of Connecticut just like we are."

"Sure! Now I remember the *Escape*! I know where they went," Stubby said. "And I ain't surprised you ain't heard from 'em. Why, they wanted to go down in them li'l ol' islands south o' Haiti and the Dominican Republic where nobody lives."

"That's them, all right," Track said. "When they want to get away, they don't fool around."

"I din't chart 'em no exact course, though. But I did tell 'em to call in at the Queen Anne Yacht Club in Kingston, Jamaica," Stubby said. "You foller their lead and you're sure to run into 'em sooner or later. But I gave 'em some advice on side trips. I'd be happy to do the same fer y'all, too."

"I hope it's no trouble," Sir Abner said.

"Why, none at all," Stubby assured him. He reached over and slapped Marvin Leroy hard on the shoulder. "Git their order ready while I set 'em straight to find they friends, boy."

"Yes, sir, Uncle Stubby," Marvin Leroy said happily. He took out a piece of paper and pencil from under the counter. After licking the pencil, he prepared to write. "Now what do y'all need for the trip?"

2

Stubby Boudreaux and Marvin Leroy Firpo stood on the dock and watched the luxury craft sail into the growing light of dawn.

Marvin Leroy waved at the figure of the crewman on stern. He turned to his uncle. "They was nice folks on the *Fancy Free*, wasn't they? And that lady was right perty, too!"

"Sure, sure," Stubby said shoving a stogie between his brown teeth. "Let's git on back to the store. There's somethin' I want you to do."

"I can guess what it is!" Marvin Leroy sang out as they walked off the dock. "I can guess what it is!"

Stubby stopped and looked at his large nephew. "Goddamn, boy! I swear you ain't got the mind of a stunned jackass! You really piss me off sometimes, know that?"

Marvin Leroy hung his head, pouted and said, "I din't do nothin', Uncle Stubby." He glanced shyly at the short man. "I'm sorry. What'd I do?"

"Yo're actin' stupid, boy," Stubby said, resuming the walk up to the store. "You ain't got the slightest damn idea o' what kinda chore there is for you."

"Yes, I do, Uncle Stubby!" Marvin Leroy crowed. "You want me to go see Pedro."

Stubby stopped again. He pulled the cigar from his mouth. "Damn! That's right. How'd you know?"

"'Cause ever'time a fancy-pants boat leaves here, you send a note to Pedro," Marvin Leroy said.

Stubby took off his cap and smacked Marvin Leroy across the face several times. "Goddamn it, shithead! Don't you ever talk 'bout me, boats and Pedro in the same sentence!"

Marvin Leroy's mouth turned down. "Yes, sir, Uncle Stubby."

The two continued the walk to the store. When they got there, Leroy Marvin asked shyly, "What's a sentence, Uncle Stubby?"

Stubby laughed to himself and shook his head. "That's what I'll get if I'm ever caught." He laughed again. "Providin' the judge is lenient!"

THE ORGANIZATION HAD NO OFFICIAL NAME. The members simply referred to themselves as The Consortium.

It was a multinational group of insurance underwriters, involved with investments in thousands of enterprises throughout the world where protection or backup was needed in the case of losses. Although none of the member companies was even near the brink of financial disaster, they all carried policies and had contingency arrangements should certain losses be forced upon them. Naturally, if their operating and investment capital was threatened, they wanted the risk removed as quickly as possible.

Often this protection could be accomplished through international diplomatic channels. If a certain nation's policies threatened the financial investment of an insured party—in the area of fishing rights, for example—then pressures were applied by gentlemen in pin-striped suits who carried attaché cases. All quite proper and lawful.

Treaties and agreements were correctly drawn up, signed and sealed to everyone's satisfaction.

However, if a nation's greed was the issue—a tinhorn dictator threatening to nationalize certain industries, for example—then the negotiations were shadier and were handled by rougher men who carried suitcases full of cash. A bit improper and *extra*legal. Money changed hands under the proverbial table, and again, everyone was satisfied.

But if neither of these methods was appropriate, a third type of negotiation was available that used the tactics of mayhem, sabotage, retaliation and violence. The Consortium had specialists to handle this end of the business, too: Track and Company. With diplomacy and bribery ruled out, Dan Track and his friends moved in to put things right with courage, cunning and weapons. No holds barred; no quarter asked or given; one side satisfied.

Sir Abner Chesterton was the contact between Dan Track and The Consortium. He delivered instructions, money and other needed items to get nasty jobs done. While his lineage placed him with the upper crust and socially elite, Sir Abner had been known to get his own hands dirty in the past.

Sir Abner was Lord of Chesterton, having inherited a few hundred acres and a manor house that had been in his family for twenty generations. Born in the 1920s, he seemed destined for a career in government or business. The young man chose the latter, going into insurance, a decision that pleased his father very much. The sire, with a captaincy in an elite territorial battalion of the Grenadier Guards, was a typical upper-class Briton—snobbish, proud and brave to the core of his English soul.

At the outbreak of the Second World War, with all the young men called to serve King and Country, Lord Chesterton had arranged for a commission for his son in the Brigade of Guards—the Grenadier Guards, of course—but Abner, a real grubber at heart, had enlisted in the Royal Commandos. His father was enraged. Not only had his son rejected his regiment, but the lad was also "mucking about in the *other ranks*, with those enlisted fellows who were supposed to follow—not lead."

Abner's eventual acceptance in the officers' training program and his ultimate commission did much to soften the blow, but not enough. Father and son were estranged until the Dieppe raid, the disastrous commando mission into Nazi-occupied France that was magnificent in its defeat. The raiders, who lost 3,350 men out of five thousand, were brave and tenacious, but could not overcome superior numbers or an impossible situation.

Abner was one of the survivors who returned to England. He arrived back, wounded but walking, and stepped onto the dock at a Royal Navy station to find Lord Chesterton there, waiting. When he spotted Abner, a bloody bandage around his head, helping take wounded survivors off a shell-pocked landing barge, the old man had broken from the crowd of officers he was with and had rushed to embrace his son.

Two years later, Lord Chesterton had fallen on a field of honor in North Africa and the title had passed to Abner.

At the end of the war Captain Abner, Lord Chesterton, was demobbed with the rest of the army. He dutifully returned to the manor house to take up the family responsibilities. A close examination of the estate, along with a rather sobering meeting with the family solicitor, revealed that Abner's father had spent more time at soldiering, hunting and gentlemanly activities than at tending to the running of the family business.

Abner tidied things up as best he could, then began to fill in the financial gap by returning to work in the insurance industry. By 1950 he had established himself as a shrewd financier in the underwriting establishment, and he was offered several temporary government postings by the Chancellor of the Exchequer to help shore up an economy in upheaval after the devastation of war.

For his services, Queen Elizabeth had knighted Abner. Although he was always comfortable with the title Lord Chesterton, he was proud to be called *Sir* Abner.

After several years in the insurance game, Abner was bored and was seriously considering retiring to the family manor and spending the rest of his days seeking adventure financed by his self-made fortune.

But it was not to be.

The Consortium called. In these increasingly turbulent times, they needed a brave chap to deal with the threats to their investments. Sir Abner's commando background suited him perfectly to take over as Director of Outside Functions. As DOF he was able to "muck about" with the sort of men he had led as a commando. He worked mostly as an S-3, a military operations officer, planning and directing the missions to remove problems that irritated The Consortium.

He'd met Dan Track after the American had volunteered to remedy a situation involving IRA terrorists in London's famous Marchand's Department Store. Dan had moved in, neutralized the bad guys and rescued the hostages. Sir Abner had wasted no time in conscripting Track to be The Consortium's troubleshooter.

The *Fancy Free* and the cover names and story were part of a Consortium mission. Marine insurers had been losing millions on numerous disappearances of expensive pleasure boats in a region of the Florida and Caribbean water known as the Spanish Main. Months of investigation and countless contacts with underworld snitches had uncovered the fact that gangs of dope smugglers were raiding these craft. After murdering all on board, these modern pirates used the boats to run controlled substances up and down the coast of Florida. Any hint that the Coast Guard had "made" the vessel, and it was sunk. The turnover was fast and the acquisition of replacement vessels for the fleet was deadly.

The *Fancy Free* was not the usual Gulfstar Motor Yacht. Equipped with twin Caterpillar 3208N diesel engines, each of which generated 210 horsepower, she had a luxury exterior. The Gulfstar was known to be equally sumptuous below deck. But this one was built for business, not pleasure.

The *Fancy Free*'s interior had been ripped out. The bulkheads had been reinforced with three layers of military surplus flak jackets. Track had wanted protection without the added weight of armor. A miniature armory, complete with ammo storage, extra weapons and repair facilities, was installed amidships below decks.

Since there was a very real possibility that they would have to entertain visitors aboard, the afterdeck had been left in its original state, complete with carpeting, expensive furnishings and bar. A guest would assume that the remainder of the vessel was typical of any yacht in the $199,000 range.

Sleeping and eating facilities were actually quite Spartan. Any self-respecting nineteenth-century fo'c'sle dweller would have sneered at the bunks. The meals were going to be plain and quickly prepared. The only gourmet food aboard would be saved for special guests. Nobody expected to gain weight from the cuisine Track had laid on.

The navigation and communication equipment was state of the art. The radar, though small, was good enough for their purposes. It was, like the flak vests, military surplus; the screen was just forward of the armory and was where George Beegh would spend much of his time.

Having sailed out of the marina on Key Largo, Zulu stood the helm watch while Sir Abner and Track carefully charted the course laid out for them by Stubby Boudreaux. They faithfully followed the route of the ill-fated *Escape to Paradise*.

MARVIN LEROY FIRPO, unhappily wearing shoes for a change, stepped off the bus and walked through the Hobart Greyhound Station. He continued on to the cab stand and stepped into the first available taxi.

The cab driver raised his eyebrows at the size of his passenger. "Where to, boy?"

"Take me here, if you please," Marvin Leroy said with a grin. He handed over the note that Stubby had written for him.

The cabbie looked at it. "Shi-yut! You hang around in tough parts, don't you, boy?"

Marvin Leroy laughed. "Yup."

The driver swung out into traffic and made a left turn onto the main drag. "You know what kinda place yo're goin' to, boy?"

"Yes, sir. I been there before."

The driver sighed. "Okay."

The boulevard narrowed to two lanes. Another left turn took them down to a section of town that was gaudy with brightly painted signs in Spanish and French. The driver stopped. "I don't take this hack o' mine no farther, boy."

"Haw!" Marvin Leroy guffawed. "None o' y'all ever do." He searched in his pockets and pulled out a carefully rolled bill. "My uncle says to give you this." He paused and looked serious. "He says if you try to git any more outta me, I's supposed to bust yore face."

"Hey, boy! Ever'thing's fine! Don't you worry."

"Yes, sir." Marvin Leroy got out of the cab. He waved goodbye to the departing vehicle, then turned to walk down the street. From the looks he attracted from passersby, it was obvious to the departing cabbie that the big kid was known in the area.

Marvin Leroy reached a bar and stepped out into the street and looked up at the sign over it. He laboriously read the words: Cantina del Cielo Cubano.

"'Ey, Marvin Leroy!" a heavily Spanish-accented voice called from the interior. "You know this place. Why don' you come on in, 'ey?"

He walked into the bar. "Howdy, Pedro."

A short, muscular Cuban wearing an unbuttoned short-sleeved shirt and khaki shorts grinned at him from the stool where he sat. "How you doing, Marvin Leroy?"

"I'm fine, thank you kindly. Uncle Stubby says to give you this." He produced a folded sheet of paper from the depth of one of his overall pockets.

"Ah!" Pedro said. *"A ver pues."* He motioned Marvin Leroy to sit at the bar. "You want a beer this time?"

"Naw," Marvin Leroy said. "I'd be obliged if'n I could have a nice cold Co'cola."

"Sure t'ing, Marvin Leroy." Pedro snapped his fingers at the bartender. *"Una Coca para el chamacote."* He sat down at the bar and opened the note. After carefully poring over the badly scribbled message for several long moments, he finally understood it. "The name of this boat is *Fancy Free*?"

Marvin Leroy grinned. "Yup."

Pedro grinned back. "*Muy bien*. Sounds like what we're looking for."

3

Track kept the *Fancy Free*'s throttles back a bit so the twin diesels remained at an easy, steady speed. The Gulfstar handled well; with a light hand on the wheel and an alert eye on the compass, he maintained the instrument's needle on south by east as the boat skirted to the north of Cuba and ploughed through the waves toward the point where he could turn south to the Windward Passage that would take him between the Communist island nation and Haiti.

It was pleasant up on the flying bridge. The early-evening breeze off the ocean had lost the heat of the day. The western sky was pinking, and the fast-growing tropical darkness in the east was threatening to close in at any time.

Track sensed movement behind him. He saw Desiree Goth's reflection in the venturi windshield. Even that distorted image showed off her beauty. Desiree wore a loose-fitting red cotton blouse, tight khaki shorts and a pair of Adidas. She walked up beside him and slipped her arm around his waist. "It is beautiful, *non*?" she remarked. She slowly withdrew her arm and turned to look back at their wake in the darkening sea.

"What? The ocean?" Track asked.

"The ocean, the sky, the weather—everything," Desiree said. She spoke in a lilting accent with the peculiar inflection of a person who has crossed many international borders and cultures. Although Stubby Boudreaux had recognized the French in her, Desiree was as mysterious as she was beautiful. She looked at Dan who stood shirtless, his bronzed, muscled torso flexing now and then as he moved the wheel or adjusted the throttles. She purred and leaned against him. "Of course I think everything is beautiful when I am with you."

Track smiled. "Careful! You'll get me all worked up. Remember the sleeping arrangements below aren't private."

"You designed the interior of our sturdy ship," she said accusingly.

"We have a job to do," Track said flatly. "And I don't let booze or pussy—"

"Bête!" Desiree said angrily. She slapped his arm so hard that a bright, cherry-red spot appeared momentarily. "I have told you, I do not like being talked to like I am a tart. Pussy, eh? See if you get any of that from me!" She stalked back to the ladder and quickly descended to aft-deck salon below.

Track grinned. He liked her temper. It was one part of the many things that attracted him to Desiree. He knew he loved the woman, yet he recognized that he was not equipped to have a permanent relationship with anyone. Desiree had a large part of his heart, he admitted, but not all of it.

Another visitor suddenly appeared. This one was much larger and even more muscular than Track. "I just saw Desiree, Major," Zulu said. "She appears to be angry."

"My crude tongue has got me in the doghouse again," Track said.

"That is easy enough with a woman," Zulu said. He spread a chart out on the control console between the wheel and the clutches. "We have made a radio fix on our position, Major," he said. "You will have to change course to south by southwest within a quarter of an hour."

"What's our schedule for hitting the Jamaica Channel?" Track asked.

"Day after tomorrow," Zulu said. "By the way, it is time for me to relieve you at the helm."

"Very well, Zulu. Take it," Track said, stepping aside and letting the big black man take over.

"Sir Abner is below with some hot English tea," Zulu said.

"I think I'll have a smoke up here in the fresh air first," Track said. He reached over and retrieved his pack of Cuesta Rey Six-T cigars.

Zulu winced. "Do us a favor, please, Major, and stay downwind."

Track laughed. "My God, Zulu! You're an Oxford graduate. Didn't you learn to enjoy the finer things of life—like good tobacco?"

"Of course I did, Major," Zulu said. "Which is exactly why I am requesting that you position yourself with care."

Track lit up and walked back to the companion bench seat at the rear of the flying bridge. He looked at the darkening sky and the hazy far horizon.

Somewhere over there he and his friends had a rendezvous with trouble. He took a pull on the stogie and slowly, thoughtfully exhaled the smoke. Despite his outward appearance of calm, Track was already tensing in anticipation of whatever awaited him. He was gut wary, and as he listened to the rhythmic throb of the prow cutting through the waves, he realized that the *Fancy Free* was being outraced by his heart.

PHILIPPE MATAMORE STOOD ON THE VERANDA of the
mansion and sipped beer from the frosted glass. He was a
tall, slim black man whose cold eyes were hidden by the
dark, wraparound glasses he always wore. A pencil-thin
mustache adorned his upper lip. His studied aloofness
contributed to his mythic reputation for having a cobra's
heart. As a member of Haiti's secret police, the near
mystical Tonton Macoutes, he was indeed as deadly as any
poisonous snake.

A nervous, fawning man stepped from the house.
"Monsieur Matamore, *s'il vous plaît*."

Without speaking, Matamore turned slowly and looked
down at the newcomer.

The uneasy fellow, also a Haitian, spoke haltingly.
"Everything is ready."

With barely a nod of his head, Matamore followed the
man into the house. The mansion was on a plantation that
had been owned by French overlords who had been mas-
sacred by their slaves in the great Haitian revolution of
1804. It had fallen to ruin, had been restored countless
times and was in varying states of repair on each of its
three floors.

Matamore strolled out onto the back porch. Another
man, this one much more sure of himself than the first,
stepped up smartly and stood at attention. Matamore ignored him, looking down at a bound prisoner who knelt
at the bottom of the steps.

Other men stood around in the yard among the over-
grown weeds and rubbish. They were a mixture of races
and nationalities, some Hispanics, others blacks who
spoke either Spanish or the Creole French of Haiti. An air
of expectancy bound the group together despite the diver-
sity of its members.

Matamore held out his hand and the man by the door placed a cocked and loaded Obregon .45 automatic pistol in it. Matamore walked down to the prisoner and looked at him.

The captive raised his face and silently pleaded with his eyes. Matamore raised the pistol and slowly pushed it against the man's head, positioning the muzzle directly between his eyes. He held it there for more than thirty seconds.

Then he squeezed the trigger.

The prisoner's head snapped back and the back of his skull cracked open, spewing out bloody brains. He was dead before his twisted body hit the broken sidewalk on which he'd been kneeling. Matamore handed the pistol back, then ascended the steps. At the top he stopped and turned and looked at the other men. They were silent and unmoving.

Matamore was satisfied. It had been a fine disciplinary lesson. Thievery, in their particular line of work, could not be tolerated, and those who committed such a crime had to be dealt quick and sure punishment.

TRACK WENT DOWN THE LADDER to the afterdeck salon. His nephew, George Beegh, sat on the deck swabbing out the tube of a PZF44 rocket launcher. The twenty-five-year-old veteran from United States Air Force intelligence displayed an easy grin. "This is one sweet baby."

Track, standing beside the heavy table that dominated the center of the compartment, wasn't impressed. "I haven't seen it in action yet—*real* action, that is."

George shrugged. "Maybe not. But I had a chance for some practice, and I'm happy with this beauty. I can throw out an 81 mm rocket with an effective range of two hundred yards. Let one of those pirates close in on us and his poop deck will end up just north of his balls."

Sir Abner Chesterton, standing in the companionway leading to the lower deck, chuckled. "I say, would you listen to the lad throwing about nautical talk? Poop deck in the balls, hey? Sounds frightfully painful."

Track laughed. "A regular Barnacle Bill, isn't he?"

George took the ribbing good-naturedly. "C'mon, you guys! I just discovered I'm a natural-born sailor. Hell, I should've run off to sea years ago." He raised the weapon to his shoulder and sighted it out the stern, tracking an imaginary enemy. "C'mon, Long John Silver! Show the Jolly Roger and I'll scuttle your butt, you one-legged bastard! I'll send you to Davy Jones's Locker with a shaped charge up your salty ass!"

Sir Abner and Track laughed so hard that Desiree walked back from the forward stateroom to see what was so funny. "Has a party started without me?"

Sir Abner stepped aside to allow her to enter the salon. "The lad is turning into a veritable Blackbeard the Pirate."

"Merde!" Desiree exclaimed with a dirty look at Track. "That is all we need around here. Another swaggering lout!" She abruptly left to return to the bow.

"Oh, dear," Sir Abner said. "It would appear that you've put our Desiree into a rather bad mood."

"Yeah," Track said. "Maybe I'd better have a word with her." He walked to the companionway and stepped onto the ladder leading to the lower deck. He continued forward until he found Desiree sitting in the forepeak. This would be George's fighting position. A rack of two dozen 81 mm rockets was already set up and waiting there.

Track stood in the doorway looking at her. "I think we better talk."

She shrugged.

"I'm sorry for being so crude up on the flying bridge. I don't mean it when I say those things to you. It's almost like I'm trying to pick a fight. I'm afraid there's a conflict building up between us," he said. "If we don't sort it out soon, this mission is going to deteriorate into a mess."

"Perhaps we have seen too much of each other," Desiree suggested. "After all, we have been together constantly for almost a month, ever since you came off that Apache reservation."

"I love you, Desiree."

"And I love you. So?"

"So our love is not a normal one," Track said. "Our work together demands dedication without outside interference or interests. The lust we feel for each other and, even worse—the caring—could easily distract us from that work, and you know that distraction could be fatal."

Desire sighed. Then she looked up at Track and smiled. "Yes—yes, you are right. That is why you arranged the boat so we would not sleep together, *n'est-ce pas*?"

"Yes," Track admitted. "Strangely enough, if we made love it would do more to increase, rather than decrease, the sexual tension between us."

"What are we going to do about it?" Desiree asked.

"I don't know," Track said. He stared at her for a few moments, then abruptly walked back through the lower deck and up to the salon. Sir Abner and George looked up from the rocket launcher. Track nodded to them. "I'm going to take the helm watch."

George was puzzled. "It's not—"

"Goddamn it! I know it's not my watch!" Track went to the ladder and climbed up to the flying bridge where Zulu stood at the wheel. "I'm taking over."

Zulu, an intelligent, perceptive man, sensed the uneasiness in his companion. "Of course, Major. This will give me an excellent opportunity to take another radio fix."

"Good idea," Track said, taking the wheel.

He settled into his solitude after Zulu left. Forcing Desiree from his mind, Track turned all thoughts to the mission ahead. Although the enterprise was completely mercenary—for the principals as well as their agents—his own personal involvement was emotional.

A quick but thorough investigation had been made of the latest disappearance. The voyage taken by the Monroes and Hamiltons aboard the *Escape to Paradise* had been minutely traced. Track and Company sailed the *Fancy Free* on the same route, calling at the same ports in an effort either to find the missing vessel and its occupants, or to corner whoever had interrupted its voyage.

One more place remained to go—Kingston, Jamaica. If there was no information there, Track and Company would be searching blind.

Although Track had never met the two couples, a background check had shown that they were decent, law-abiding and generous people who gave much of their time and efforts to helping others whose places in the world were much less secure than their own.

Now there was a good chance the Monroes and Hamiltons had been murdered and their boat stolen. The thought of it enraged Track. These sleazy dope runners catered to the desires and needs of the emotionally and spiritually crippled who depended on chemicals to get them through life. Track wondered if any of the users ever considered where their money went or how much blood was spilled so that they could snort, shoot and smoke their way into an artificial dreamworld.

Street junkies, society people or sports heroes, all users shared a perception of the real world as phony and jaded as that of their own real worth.

Track and Company was about to eliminate some of the suppliers and nuke the dreamworld of a few thousand dopers.

4

With Zulu at the helm, the *Fancy Free* sailed into Kingston harbor at midday. The husky black man handled the vessel like a fine-tuned instrument as he deftly wound his way through the crowded waters that bordered the famous tropical city.

Track, following Stubby Boudreaux's advice, had made use of the ship-to-shore radio and arranged berthing facilities at the Queen Anne Yacht Club—as the people aboard the *Escape to Paradise* had done. In fact, he had claimed the Eastport Yacht Club of Stamford, Connecticut, as the *Fancy Free*'s home port. It was the same place from where the Hamiltons and Monroes had sailed several weeks previously.

Although their arrival seemed no different from the hundreds of others in Jamaica, there was one thing that made it unique. Through The Consortium's considerable influence, the *Fancy Free* had been able to avoid customs. Any close inspection of the vessel would have proved awkward, given the weaponry and munitions aboard.

Thus, Zulu was able to go directly into the marina of the Queen Anne Yacht Club.

A rather dashing gentleman, complete with a docking team, stood at the slip obviously waiting for the *Fancy Free*. It appeared that he and Sir Abner had been cut from the same cloth. Slim, tall, with a neatly clipped military mustache and standing straight as a musket barrel, the stranger doffed his yachting cap to Desiree who stood on the foredeck in front of the flying bridge.

"Good morning to you, madam, and welcome to Kingston," he said in a regal British upper-class accent. "We've received your wireless broadcast and have been waiting for you."

Desiree, wearing cutoffs, sneakers and a halter, waved to him. "Thank you."

The Englishman stepped aside gracefully to allow the two young black men with him to attend to tying the *Fancy Free* to the dock. When they had finished, he approached the vessel. He glanced up at Zulu standing at the wheel on the flying bridge. "Permission to come aboard?"

"Of course, sah," Zula called down affecting an accent that could be best described as a combination of West Indian and African. His usual Oxford manner of speech would hardly fit the role he was playing. "I am Cap'n Baharia."

"A most appropriate name," the man said. "Means 'sailor' in Swahili, what?"

"Yes, sah," Zulu said, a bit nonplussed by the man's knowledge. "The men of my family have always been seagoin' fellahs out of Nigeria."

"Jolly good! Seen a spot of Africa meself," the Englishman said, stepping aboard. "I am Commodore Durham-Jones of the Queen Anne Yacht Club."

"The owner is below, sah," Zulu said. "He should be on deck presently."

"Certainly," Durham-Jones said, smiling. "I shan't mind waiting." He walked along the side deck to join Desiree on the foredeck. Once again he doffed his cap. "May I repeat the pleasure of wishing you a good morning, madam?"

"Of course," Desiree said. "I am Mrs. Hunter."

"Charmed," Durham-Jones said. He took her hand and kissed it lightly. "Commodore Durham-Jones at your service." He chuckled. "Actually I am a retired lieutenant-commander of the Royal Navy, but my elected position in the club allows me the pretense of using a more inflated rank."

"And you suit it well," Desiree said.

"Oh, madam!" Durham-Jones exclaimed. "You are as much a flatterer as you are beautiful."

Desiree instantly liked the older gentleman. He was as corny as a B-picture matinee idol, yet he had a charm about him that was as disarming as it was delightful. She saw Sir Abner and Track appear on the flying bridge. "Ah, there is my husband with his uncle."

Durham-Jones turned and looked up at Track. "Are you the incredibly lucky Mr. Hunter?"

Track frowned in puzzlement. "Lucky?"

The Englishman laughed. "Of course, dear fellow! To be married to such a lovely lady." He gestured toward Desiree with a gallant sweep of his hand. Desiree curtsied, then looked up at Track and, noting that the Briton was looking the other way, stuck her tongue out at her lover.

Track grinned. "I'm lucky, all right. I can't argue with that."

Sir Abner waved to his countryman. "Would you join us for a spot of early tea?"

"Delighted!"

Five minutes later, in the afterdeck salon, Desiree did the honors of making introductions. "This is Commodore Durham-Jones," she said, "a gentleman of rare quality and sensitivity." She looked directly at Track as she spoke.

"Oh, dear!" Durham-Jones said. "Mrs. Hunter is too kind, believe me."

After the others were introduced, George Beegh served hot tea and a tray of store-bought cookies. George was dressed in a striped nautical-type T-shirt and a pair of U.S. Navy bell-bottom trousers. His bare feet were shoved into white deck shoes.

Durham-Jones was impressed. "Good Lord! He's a sailor and accomplished servant, too!"

George smiled modestly, then set the tray of cookies on the table. Despite the genteel appearance of the compartment, there were some decidedly deadly items efficiently stowed out of sight in various crannies. Among these were George's surplus rockets for the PZF44 rocket launcher, two Uzi submachine guns, Sir Abner's 9 mm Sterling, shrapnel and concussion grenades, first-aid equipment and plenty of ammunition. All were in reach and out of sight.

Commodore Durham-Jones settled down on the settee that ran the length of the bulkhead, unaware of the deadly paraphernalia beneath him.

"It's deucedly good to speak to a fellow Englishman again," Sir Abner said. "It's a bother to have half of one's family born and raised in the colonies."

Track laughed. "The colonies, Uncle? I believe I learned in school about a certain Revolutionary War that brought about the sovereignty of those colonies and changed them into the United States of America."

"Balderdash!"

Durham-Jones laughed. "I shall certainly treat that as a family argument and bow gracefully—and quickly—out!"

Track let a few minutes of light conversation slide by. Mostly it consisted of Desiree charming the socks off the old Englishman. But Track finally was able to logically work in some small talk of his own. "We called in at the

Queen Anne Yacht Club on the recommendation of some close friends.''

"Really?" Durham-Jones asked. "And who might they be?"

"The Monroes and Hamiltons," Track said. "We received a postcard from them, and finally a letter." The mail he mentioned had actually been sent to other persons, but had been made available as part of the investigation of the two couples' disappearance. "They mentioned you, Commodore."

"Oh, dear, let me think—" Durham-Jones was pensive for several moments. "I'm having a bit of trouble recalling them. Could you—oh, wait! From Connecticut, right? The Eastport Yacht Club of Stamford!"

"Those are the ones," Sir Abner said. "We're trying to find them, but they seem to have gone off somewhere out of reach. They had been directed here by a gentleman named Stubby Boudreaux."

"Ah, yes. He's a man quite charming in a—" he paused and winked at Sir Abner "—rather *colonial* fashion, what? Then I'm a bit surprised they're out of reach. Our Mr. Boudreaux usually sends that sort to us. As I now recall, the Hamiltons and Monroes were, indeed, looking for remote lonely islands to visit. I knew a few places, but nothing particularly exotic. I advised them to visit Old Arlo."

"Old Arlo?"

"Yes, indeed! Quite a character. An old Jamaican black who's been sailing these waters for at least sixty years," Durham-Jones explained. "He knows every island, inlet and lagoon on the Spanish Main. Mr. Hamilton and Mr. Monroe wasted no time in calling on him. They paid the old boy for a rather detailed chart."

Desiree's eyes lit up. "Perhaps that is what we must do."

"Of course," Durham-Jones said. "But I don't advise you to visit Old Arlo, dear lady. He resides in a rather seedy part of our waterfront. In fact, it's a bit dangerous at times for men."

"It would be worth the risk if you would be kind enough to give us directions on how to reach him," Sir Abner said. "I shan't go, however. I prefer to allow my nephew and Captain Baharia to traipse through the rough parts of town."

"Of course, Mr. Chesterton," Durham-Jones said. "But first let me stand a round of drinks in the club bar. After that you, Mrs. Hunter and I could while away a few pleasant hours while these sturdy chaps go about visiting Old Arlo. Then, later on, perhaps I could give you a bit of information on seeking out the more genteel and entertaining parts of Kingston."

Desiree turned on the charm. "It would be lovely if you would accompany us on such an evening, Commodore."

"Of course! So nice of you to invite me," Durham-Jones said. He stood up. "But first! Time for a gin and tonic. Take it from an Englishman. It is the only fit drink for white men in the tropics." He looked at Sir Abner. "What, Chesterton?"

"Ra-ther!" Sir Abner replied, beaming.

THE RADIO OPERATOR LAID HIS PENCIL ASIDE and took the earphones off his head. After giving the message he'd just received a cursory glance, he left the squalid, cramped communications room and walked through the mansion to the back porch.

Philippe Matamore, as was his custom, stood at the railing sipping his beer. He gazed seaward in a long reverie that was broken only by occasionally turning his attention to the rich, dark bottle of Miragoane beer.

"Señor Matamore," the radio operator called out. He displayed little of the fear others showed around Matamore. The commo man had a powerful skill, able not only to interpret the mysterious dits-and-dahs of the Morse code that came in from the air to visit his receiver-transmitter, but also to broadcast messages sending communications out the same way. Among the Haitians in the group, his craft was considered close to magic.

Matamore slowly turned and silently waited to hear whatever the operator had to say.

"Pedro from Florida has contacted us about a possible boat," the man said. "It should be on the *El Mar Grande Español* this week."

Matamore's only sign of pleasure was a slight nod of his head. *"Bien,"* he said in the Creole French of his homeland. *"Comment s'appelle le bateau?"*

"No le comprendo," the Spanish-speaking radioman said, indicating his ignorance of the Haitian tongue.

Matamore slipped into the other's language. *"¿Cómo se llama el barco?"*

"Fancy Free," the radioman answered.

Again Matamore nodded. "We shall be ready."

Then he turned back to his beer.

OLD ARLO'S FACE WAS AS PUCKERED and wrinkled as a dried apple sprinkled with coal dust. His bloodshot eyes, blasted by years of ocean spray and tropical sun, had once been sharp enough to discern the shadowy outlines of an island on any horizon no matter how far away it was.

Now all he had was the memory of what he had once been able to see. But the skills of the true seaman and navigator were still strong in his ancient heart.

Track and Zulu sat in Arlo's shack at a crude table opposite the old mariner. A surly young black man, leaning against the far wall, gazed unsmilingly at the strangers. The men were in a typical dock shanty that sported a tar paper roof to keep out the sudden showers so typical of the tropics. One side of the structure was open enough to allow a bit of a breeze to waft through and relieve the heat.

Following Durham-Jones's good advice, Track and Zulu had shown up with more than just cash to pay for the old sailor's counsel; they had brought several bottles of strong Jamaican rum with them.

Arlo sipped some of the thick, fiery liquid between his toothless gums, swallowing greedily. Any other man, even one much younger, would have been staggered by the sudden onslaught of alcohol on his system. But Arlo only exhaled in pleasure as he sat the bottle down.

"Good rum, mon," he announced. "Mek a warm belly like a woman. Now I am too old for woman—so I take to rum."

Zulu smiled. "We have brought you plenty, Arlo."

Arlo nodded, then gestured behind him. "Dis be my nephew Harry. Don' give him not'in'—I don' lak him no ways."

If the nephew felt any emotional pull from his uncle's unkind words, he did not show it. He maintained his unfriendly glare.

Arlo squinted at his visitors. "And what would you gennelmen want of old Arlo?"

Track leaned forward. "We're looking for friends of ours named Monroe and Hamilton. You gave them directions to get to lonely, isolated islands. They wanted to explore and do some snorkeling and fishing." He made ready to go into a lengthy explanation to jog the old man's memory, but Arlo's brain was as alert as ever.

"I 'member your frien's, mon," he said. "Want to go where nobody else ever sail on dat Spanish Main." He laughed. "But I tell dem it is no possible. Ol' Arlo, he already sail ever'where, mon!"

"Then you can remember where you told those people they should go?" Zulu asked.

"Sure t'ing, Cap'n. I send dem to where dat Jamaican Channel spill into Caribbean Sea. Dat ol' channel, him a differ'nt color from de Caribbean Sea. Lot's of folks no can see, but ol' Arlo he see. I know de place. When I was a young mon, I take my boat dere allatime. Lots o' islands, mon! But dem 'merican fellahs need numbahs. I show 'em on de map and they write down numbahs."

"Can you show us on the chart?" Track asked. "We'll be happy to pay you."

"You got 'merican monies, mon?"

"Sure," Track said. "What's your price?"

Arlo's weak eyes could barely make out the case of rum on the floor beside him. He pointed to it. "I take dem rums and five dollah, mon."

Harry, the nephew, interrupted. "Make dat fifteen dollahs, mon!" There was a cross between a sneer and a threat in his voice.

"Don' lissen to him," Arlo protested. "I'm no greedy mon."

"Fifteen is fine," Track said. He nudged Zulu. "Pay him, Captain Baharia."

Zulu slid the money across the table.

"You got dat map?" Arlo said.

"Yes," Track answered.

"Get him out, mon." Arlo got up and wobbled across the small room to a shelf. He returned with a large magnifying glass. After Track spread the map out on the table, the old man studied the chart through the lens. Finally he laid his finger on a spot. "You go dere, mon. Find lotsa little islan's, mon. An' your frien's dey go dere, too."

Track carefully put a mark where Arlo had laid his finger. "We'll work out a fix back on the *Fancy Free*," he said to Zulu.

Arlo cackled. "Numbahs, 'ey? Damn dem numbahs, mon! Look for de change of color in dat water, mon!"

Zulu laid a friendly hand on the old man's bony shoulder. "We couldn't do that, Arlo. We're not as good at sailing as you are."

"I sail ol' ocean t'ousand times," Arlo said seriously. "He try to kill me, but I make peace wit' him so he let me come home." He turned his wizened face up to peer at them. He seemed to sense something in Track. He stood up so he could put his face close to the American's. Then Arlo shook his head. "You same lak my nephew Harry—you don't need peace wit' de ocean, mon. You need peace wit' yoself."

"Sometimes that's hard to do," Track said.

"De Spanish Main knows your kind, mon," Arlo said seriously. "He take you to de bottom and mix your bones wit' dem ol' pirates."

Zulu said softly. "If God wills it."

Harry spoke insolently. "Dey no God on de Spanish Main, mon!"

Arlo nodded his head. "Harry be right, mon! God forsake de Spanish Main four hunnerd years ago!"

5

The loud music blasted out of the natural megaphone of the lagoon entrance and carried across the open waters of the ocean with crystal clarity.

The leader of the raiders, his fingers idly beating in time with the rock number, peered over the bow of the motor launch into the twilight's gloom. He smiled with satisfaction. It had been extremely easy to find the boat identified to them as the *Fancy Free*.

The idiot aboard the craft had blabbered like a magpie into his radio transmitter asking for anyone within range of his broadcasts to answer him and chat for a while. The leader chuckled. It was almost as if the man had been begging to be found. The raiders' mother ship, a sleek cabin cruiser now anchored a couple of hundred yards away, had simply homed its radio-tracking beacon onto the ceaseless babbling and let it veer them to it.

The coxswain, in the stern of the small auxiliary craft, pushed on the tiller, turning the boat toward the lagoon opening that was canopied by the overlapping palms of coconut trees. He twisted the throttle to slow down the outboard motor.

The leader turned his head around. "Keep the speed up!" he snapped.

The coxswain protested. "They will hear us."

"Not over all that music," the leader said.

The coxswain shrugged. *"Tienes razón."*

In addition to the leader and coxswain, there were two other men in the launch. All were well armed with handguns and knives.

Finally the motor was cut, and the momentum carried the boat into the lagoon where the source of the music was readily visible. It was a motor yacht, all its lights extinguished except those in the main cabin located below deck in front of the afterdeck salon. A party was obviously in progress.

The leader saw the name on the stern. He pronounced it out loud, reading it phonetically in his native Spanish language. "Fahn-cee Fray-ay."

Across twenty yards of water, peering out a porthole at the approaching attackers, Track looked forward and waved a warning to George Beegh. George crouched in the doorway of the forepeak. The PZF44 rocket launcher, armed and ready, leaned against the bulkhead. George held a new AR-15 9 mm rifle in his hands. He acknowledged Track's signal with a wink.

Track turned the other way, glancing up to the afterdeck salon. Desiree Goth, the Uzi submarine gun fully loaded, nodded back at him. Zulu, also holding an Uzi and positioned farther aft, gave a little wave.

Sir Abner, beside Track, cradled a Sterling submachine gun. Despite his companions' vehement arguments that there were handier, more compact combat firearms available, the stubborn Englishman insisted on arming himself with that particular brand of weapon. "I carried its grandfather, the Sten, in the Commandos," he argued, "and I'm quite handy with it." Then he added almost haughtily, "Of course you must also take into account that it's British!"

Track's own choice was his tried and proven Franchi SPAS-12 combat shotgun. With the folded stock pushed in and alternating loads of solid slug and buckshot, the weapon was ready for action.

There was barely a splash or bump as the intruders came alongside the *Fancy Free*. The leader's head appeared briefly above the gunwale, then disappeared again. Seconds later he slithered aboard, followed by two other men. They crept silently to the entrance of the afterdeck salon and waited.

Track took a breath and yelled loud enough to be heard above the music, "Hey, George! Gimme 'nother drink, huh?"

George, making his voice sound slurred and drunk, called back. "Sure thing. Wanna a vodka drink or a Scotch drink or what?"

"Make it a Seagram's," Track said. He only had time to glance up at the doorway and note that both Desiree and Zulu had pulled back out of harm's way.

The leader of the raiders, satisfied that there was nothing but a party of drunks to deal with, boldly stepped onto the ladder leading to the lower deck. Track swung the muzzle of the SPAS-12 around to line up on the man's belly. The weapon belched thunder, hurtling a solid slug that caught the pirate between chest and abdomen. The sudden impact hurled the man across the salon into the after bulkhead.

Track ducked back, knowing that Desiree and Zulu would spring into action.

The pair wasted not a moment. Their Uzis barked a couple of firebursts each, hosing streams of 9 mm slugs into the second raider. He twitched under the wicked lashing and fell below decks to crash heavily at the foot of the ladder on top of his companion.

George scrambled through the hatch above his station in the forepeak in time to level the AR-15 on the third raider. His weapon sparked in the twilight and two well-spaced slugs, one hitting the man in the side above the pelvis and the second going into his skull through the ear opening, tossed the victim into the placid waters of the lagoon.

By then Sir Abner was up the ladder and in the door of the salon. His Sterling submachine gun chug-a-chugged, its steel-jacket rounds raking the launch. The boat shivered under the onslaught, and the coxswain fell over the stern into the water. He made no moves, not even a tremor, as he floated peacefully over to the other dead man in an ever-explanding crimson stain.

Sir Abner was joined on deck by the others. The Englishman was elated. "Good show, what?"

"It's not over yet," Track reminded him. "Those bastards came from another vessel."

George thought of the rocket launcher. "Let's go sink the lubber." He looked up at the growing darkness. "And we'd better move quick while it's still light enough to see."

"Aye, aye, Cap'n Kidd!" Track said with a laugh.

Zulu imitated a boatswain's whistle then called out, "General quarters! General quarters!"

George, so excited that he missed the point of the humor aimed at him, raced back to the forepeak. "Man your battle stations!"

Desiree shook her head. "A bunch of silly boys!"

But silly boys or not, everyone went to his prearranged position for the anticipated sea battle.

Sir Abner, who would be the combat helmsman, took over the control console in the main cabin. After hitting the starters, he engaged the clutches and shoved the throttles forward. A quick crank of the wheel whirled the *Fancy*

Free around, and she rapidly gained speed in the small lagoon before shooting out to the open ocean.

Track had climbed to the flying bridge. He yelled down to Sir Abner. "Hold a steady course!" It took only a few moments to spot their quarry. "Off the port bow!" Track said.

"I see her, Dan, my boy!" Sir Abner yelled. "Tallyho!"

George was caught up in the spirit. "Tally fucking ho!"

"Bloody colonial," Sir Abner complained.

"Don't forget to allow for the backblast from George's rocket," Track reminded Sir Abner. "If he fires that damned thing at the wrong angle, he can sink us, too." He looked down at his nephew. "Did you hear me? You be careful with the ass end of that thing!"

"Right, Dan," George said, hefting the tube onto his shoulder.

Three very surprised men abroad a sleek cabin cruiser watched them coming—for only a few seconds. Then the trio leaped into action. A foaming wake announced their plan to escape.

"George!" Sir Abner hollered. "Get ready for a shot!"

"I'm ready," George assured him.

Sir Abner turned to starboard, angling slightly away from the fleeing boat. George swung his launcher a few degrees to the left, took a sight picture and fired.

An orange flash marked the rocket's ignition, and it zipped from the tube and streaked across the water.

Unfortunately George's aim was a bit high and flat. The round simply streaked over the pirates' bow and hit the water on the other side, skipping like a thrown flat rock before running out of steam and unceremoniously sinking beneath the waves without so much as a bang.

"Shit!" George exclaimed. "Gimme another chance!"

"Right, old son," Sir Abner said. He turned to port this time. It was a risky maneuver, carrying them at a near ninety-degree angle to the faster boat. But at least George would have a better range of fire.

The rocket launcher was aimed. Once more there was ignition. This time the 81 mm rocket zipped across the open space, flying straight and true above the waves. It struck the fleeing boat on the starboard bow and exploded in a cherry-orange blast.

The force of the explosion pushed the cruiser off course and caused it to yaw, then skid across the water and rock violently. Sir Abner kept the *Fancy Free* on full throttle and turned back to an intercepting course.

"Hit the flying bridge, George!" Track yelled, wishing like hell they were within range to use the SPAS-12.

"Aye, aye, sir!"

Sir Abner swung slightly to starboard, then straightened out. "Fire away, lad!"

The second rocket went into the cabin just under the flying bridge. The explosion disintegrated the bridge deck and threw the boat's pilot into the air. His legs went in two crazy directions while the rest of him flew straight up in the air like a launched missile. Three separate sprays marked his splashdown in the Caribbean Sea.

Sir Abner changed course and headed straight at the cabin cruiser. Desiree and Zulu joined Track on the portside deck. George climbed through the hatch from the forepeak and got into position to cover them.

"Boarders away!" Sir Abner yelled as he drew alongside.

Track leaped across the eight feet of open space and landed on the pirates' boat. Jumping down to the cockpit, he was suddenly standing face-to-face with a grim character squatting behind the cockpit freezer.

A load of buckshot from the SPAS-12 sprayed out in a thundering blast, but the freezer soaked up most of it. The pirate, a Smith and Wesson .38 revolver in his one uninjured hand, quickly fired three rounds.

He fired too quickly. He missed Track.

Solid slug, buckshot and another solid slug pounded the pirate into human hamburger against the after bulkhead. He fell behind the freezer, the blood from his shotgun-butchered body flowing out on the deck in a thick, wide pool.

The sliding door leading into the cabin had been blown off by George's rocket. Track, with Desiree and Zulu on his heels, charged through after his buckshot calling card.

The third man lay quietly inside. From his condition it was easy to see that the PZF44 card had been received.

Zulu hurried below decks, then returned. "Nobody there, Major."

"Thank you, Zulu." He turned to Desiree. "How're you doing?"

Her eyes snapped. "I am doing fine, of course! And why shouldn't I be?"

"Christ!" Dan exclaimed. "Can't a guy just ask about—"

"In combat I am only your comrade," Desiree interrupted. "Why haven't you asked Zulu how he is? Or Sir Abner? Or George?"

Track started to reply, then stopped. Muttering "That fucking tension between us," he left her and climbed up the bent ladder to what was left of the flying bridge. "George, get over here and give Zulu a hand pouring fuel around this tub."

"Right, Dan," George said, acknowledging the order.

Track walked to the edge of the pirates' boat and leaped back aboard the *Fancy Free* to join Sir Abner on the flying bridge. "We'll burn her and let the rest of the gang wonder what happened to their boys."

"Good idea, Dan, old son," Sir Abner said. "A fine application of psychological warfare."

Track looked down and saw Desiree still standing in the cockpit. "Desiree, get back to our boat."

She looked up at him. "I will help Zulu and George."

"They don't need any help, goddamn it!" he snapped. "Get back aboard here!"

Desiree, angry, yelled back, *"Mais oui, monsieur le capitaine!"* She jumped aboard the *Fancy Free* and went into the salon.

"You're a bit short with each other, aren't you?" Sir Abner remarked.

"Sometimes that woman could piss off a saint," Track said. "Hey!" he hollered down at Zulu and George. "Don't take all fucking day!"

George looked up. "Give us a break, huh? We gotta syphon this fuel outta the tank. What the hell do you think? They've got it in handy little bottles or something?"

A quarter of an hour later, Track and Company stood aboard the *Fancy Free*. George, with the rocket launcher on his shoulder, took casual aim and fired. The round hit the pirate boat and exploded, igniting the spilled fuel.

The group watched the craft burn, the flames throwing out broad, irregular dancing beacons of light into the tropical night.

Finally, with a great hissing of steam, the cabin cruiser rolled over, then slipped beneath the waves to join other vessels that had died violent deaths on the Spanish Main.

Sir Abner looked at Track. "What to do now, my lad?"

"Back to Kingston," Track said. "We've got to let folks know we're still alive and kicking. Then we'll draw another bunch of those bastards out."

Sir Abner brought the engines to life. "Tallyho," he said under his breath.

6

Madeleine Noire awoke in the large bed. She opened her eyes to gaze up at the white gauze of the mosquito netting as she stretched her long, ebony body. The muscles rippled under the deceptive softness of rounded feminine curves. She wore the relaxation that followed a night of submission to the powerful lovemaking of her man, Philippe Matamore, like a heavy blanket.

Madeleine smiled and sighed contentedly as she recalled his powerful thrusting and the peaks of passion that had welled up in her like a hurricane-charged tide. She rolled over to embrace him and found his side of the bed empty. Alarmed by his absence, she quickly looked around the room.

"Philippe? *Mon amour!*" she called out.

Matamore stepped from the adjoining bathroom. Despite the heat and the early hour, he was dressed in slacks and a crisp white shirt. He wore expensive Italian shoes over socks of pure silk. "I have business this morning, *chérie*," he said softly as he slipped on his dark glasses. Madeleine was the only human being, other than an old aunt in Port-au-Prince, whom he showed any consideration or affection for. "Jorge's boat is not in the harbor."

It was possible to look out from their bedroom window in the old French mansion and view the anchorage where the boats of Ile-a-Salut were moored.

Madeleine slid from the bed and joined him. "Perhaps he is but tarrying," she said in a low, sexy voice. She gently pushed her limber, swaying body against him, rubbing slowly and suggestively.

"Non," Matamore said. "We needed that new boat badly. He would not be late without a good reason."

Madeleine's idea of quick seduction quickly faded. She recognized that her man's passion was always overshadowed by his work. The rewards outweighed the disappointment.

Matamore kissed her tenderly. "I will see you for luncheon."

"Oui, mon amour," Madeleine agreed, backing languidly toward the bed.

THE ISLAND NATION OF HAITI has always been one of the unhappiest spots on the face of this battered old world. Not much is known of the place before Christopher Columbus visited there in 1492.

It has been noted that he did not stay long.

The French colonized the island in 1677, establishing a cruel system of plantation life that was sustained through the brutish subjugation of a slave labor force imported from Africa. This regime ended in 1804, however, when one of those brutalized individuals, a particularly hard case named Toussaint L'Ouverture, led a bloody rebellion.

The revolution had two outstanding features: one, it succeeded, giving the Haitian people independence; two, it was one of the bloodiest struggles for freedom ever recorded, as a cruelly used populace paid back their evil masters tit for tat in murderous spasms of vengeance.

From that point on, Haiti's lot didn't improve much. Revolutions, counterrevolutions, assassinations, invasion by the U.S. Marines and other troubles pressed down on this impoverished, superstitious land.

This misery and violence was the inheritance of Philippe Matamore. He was born in the slums of Port-au-Prince, Haiti, in 1945. His father was a small-time thief, pimp and paid enforcer. His large size had enabled him to earn extra money, between shifts of selling his sister, Matamore's Aunt Charmine, and burglarizing his neighbors, by beating the hell out of people for money.

It appeared as if life would go on in that fashion forever until Dr. François "Papa Doc" Duvalier was elected president in 1957. At that time little Philippe Matamore was only twelve years old, but he was already helping his father in the family business, acting as lookout during burglaries and beatings, or roaming the streets drumming up business for Aunt Charmine.

But the creation of the Tonton Macoutes changed all that.

Papa Doc didn't trust his military. In order to ensure his safety and his tenure in office—which he decided not to risk by foolishly allowing any more elections—he needed a band of special security people. Since it was impossible to find exactly what he wanted among the more law-abiding citizenry, Papa Doc turned to those folks who lived outside the law.

He recruited the bullying thugs who terrorized the streets of the larger cities. Their primary duty was to see that he stayed securely in the president's office. This group was first known as the Cagoulards. Wearing masks, they intimidated political meetings, beating up opposition supporters. Papa Doc's strong-arm boys took on new duties and responsibilities as the years passed.

Philippe Matamore's father became a Cagoulard, and from that point the family's fortune improved. Aunt Charmine was able to stay at home. They moved into a section of town reserved for Cagoulards. During those years, Philippe began to acquire a taste for the better things of life.

Later the Cagoulards became officially known as the Tonton Macoutes. There is no agreement on the actual meaning of the name, but experts in the Creole French of Haiti believe it refers to legendary "bogeymen" who carry away folks who misbehave. In fact, many people "disappeared" at the hands of the Tontons. The law in Haiti was administered through the whims and attitudes of these thugs and killers.

With the new name came a bit more sophistication. The masks were replaced by the darkest of sunglasses. Tropical suits, complete with shirt and tie, were now worn in place of the undershirts and shorts of the past.

In 1963, when Philippe Matamore turned eighteen, he became an official member of the group. He found himself in a cellular organization without a structured command or staff system. In fact, the various section chiefs were forbidden to communicate with one another. They were required to go directly to Papa Doc in order to carry out their business and duties. It seemed that *Monsieur le Président de la République d'Haiti* did not trust his appointed bullyboy secret police.

Matamore performed well as a Tonton. The first thing he did was even up a couple of old scores, arresting and shooting a trio of street guys who had given him a hard time over some gambling debts. There was also an old woman who used to shoo him away from the front of her stall in the marketplace when he was just a kid hanging around to steal things from her. The crone, accused of plotting with revolutionaries, was thrown into a cell to starve.

After that, Matamore settled in, earning plenty of extra money as an informer. Where he couldn't find a case, he would create one, falsely accusing innocent persons of plotting against the government. His hard work was appreciated, and he was further rewarded by being placed under special tutelage to serve an apprenticeship as an interrogator. Here he developed skills in administering controlled torment when information—either real or created—was required.

He also oversaw an organization of paid civilian informants. In a nation where a maid earned less than ten dollars a month, it was not difficult to develop such a network. Witch doctors were particularly valuable in the superstitious, backward nation. These priests of black magic were privy to much that went on around them, not only in the countryside, but also in the city slums. And they, too, could be bribed to manufacture whatever evidence was required.

When Papa Doc died in 1971, his son, a portly lad named Jean-Claude "Baby Doc" Duvalier, took over. This change in leadership brought about a transition in the Tonton Macoutes, as well. With unfavorable international publicity growing, based on the testimony of expatriot Haitians, Baby Doc thought it better to reorganize state security. A paramilitary uniformed militia named the Leopards took over many of the Tontons' old jobs—in the cities.

The Tontons were renamed *Volontaires pour Securité National*—Volunteers for National Security—and moved to the boondocks where they flourished. Philippe Matamore, now a section chief, was taken from the city streets and transferred to Ile-a-Salut. His new island post put an entire district at his mercy and provided him with a rundown plantation house to use as his headquarters.

He had progressed from informer to warlord.

Contacts he had made through family, friends and professional associates had put him in intimate touch with dope runners. Under the watchful eye of his superiors and the government, he had never been able to use those contacts. Now, away from Port-au-Prince and official scrutiny, he was able to use them to his advantage.

Thirteen years after establishing himself on Ile-a-Salut, Philippe Matamore ruled a small kingdom—one as wealthy as any oil potentate's sheikhdom in the Middle East.

And he would kill to keep it.

THE RADIO OPERATOR, his feet up on the table as he read a magazine, turned as Matamore entered the room. He knew what his boss wanted. "I have heard nothing from Jorge and his bunch, *jefe*."

Matamore was "chief" in the two languages employed in his domain—*jefe* to the Spanish speakers and *chef* to the Haitians. It was part of the international flavor of the place, though the VSN man would have preferred *rey* and *roi*—"king."

"When was the last time you heard from Jorge?"

"Early last evening," the man answered. "He said they were closing in on the boat without difficulty, and he would contact me when the situation was under control. But since then, no word, *jefe*."

"It is all very strange," Matamore said. "I wonder what is delaying his return."

"Jorge is a good man," the radio operator mused. "Perhaps there is some problem with the new boat—or his own. *Así es, jefe*—mechanical problems, no doubt."

"You could be right," Matamore said. He glanced with distaste at the jumbled condition of the room. An ashtray overflowed and there were old newspapers and periodicals strewn from one corner of the floor to the other. "This place is a mess."

The operator shrugged and held up his notepad. Neat lines were written across the pages. "But this isn't, *jefe*. And that's what I'm paid to take care of."

"I'll send you a maid," Matamore said.

"*Chingado!* There are already too damn many women around here," the man said. "This place sounds like a henhouse in the evenings." Then he laughed. "Of course there's plenty of *culo* to enjoy, no?"

Matamore, interested in only one woman, merely nodded.

He walked from the radio room and out onto the porch. He paused at the head of the steps and could see the black stain left by the blood of the man he had executed. Large flies buzzed around it, still able to pick up a faint odor.

Matamore descended the wooden steps and strode through the gore into the yard, causing the insects to disperse momentarily, before going back to their endless circling flights.

An unattended grove of jungle vegetation stood between the mansion and the village. Matamore liked it this way. He felt that the natural separation maintained his aloofness and aided in maintaining discipline. His old Tonton habit of staying mysterious and away from the general population suited Philippe Matamore just fine.

As he strode through the helter-skelter arrangements of shacks toward the anchorage, he glanced at the temporary homes of the inhabitants. All, even the least educated and most crude, of his men were wealthy and had beautiful permanent homes in such places as Venezuela, Colombia, Panama and even Miami, Florida.

The shanties were expensively furnished. A series of generators fed electricity not only to Matamore's mansion but also to this small village. Television sets, washing machines, stereos and other electronic luxuries had been rowed ashore from boats in the harbor.

And there were women, too.

All races were represented here. They ran the human gamut from blondes—bleached and natural—to dusky African beauties who had grown up in the towns and cities of the Spanish Main.

They all had two things in common, however. All were lovely creatures, and all of them had been bought and paid for by their men. They came to Ile-a-Salut pouting about having to leave their big homes but soon stopped complaining. Competition was abundant and a wealthy lover might tire of a nag, replacing her in a matter of hours with a prettier or younger rival. In reality, the women of Ile-a-Salut were keeping a close eye on their life investments.

Now and then Matamore could see through an unshaded window. Sprawled together on expensive sheets, these former residents of some of the worst slums in the world had grown rich off the weaknesses and trendy pastimes of inhabitants of the wealthiest cities in the world—places like Chicago, New York, Los Angeles and Dallas.

Matamore reached a little rise and could clearly see the natural harbor. A half dozen boats rocked on their anchor cables like sleeping dogs on chains. The Tonton raised his eyes and looked out at sea.

Still no sign of Jorge.

This was something that would have to be checked out and investigated thoroughly. If Jorge had pulled a fast one, he must be found and punished as an example. If someone else had done in the pirate, then that called for action, too.

There were two words for that on Ile-a-Salut—*venganza* and *revanche*—revenge.

It was the strongest part of their code of honor.

7

The United States Coast Guard found the cabin cruiser *Escape to Paradise* a month after it had been reported lost.

Someone had made a hasty and crude attempt to scuttle the craft, but had failed. Instead of burning and sinking, the boat had drifted and had finally gently grounded itself on a sandbar off Boca Chica Key, Florida.

A preliminary examination by the Coast Guard had shown that the interior of the boat had been ripped out. There had been some skillful carpentry work done to reinforce the boat to haul heavy loads. A few loose leaves of marijuana and strands of burlap bagging were discovered. It was surmised that the odds of the *Escape*'s being identified had finally stacked against her.

The *Escape to Paradise* was pulled off the bar and towed into the Coast Guard station at Key West. A more scientific examination was conducted under the authority of United States Customs. Traces of cocaine and blood on the lower deck were turned up. A dossier had been compiled on the missing couples who had been aboard the *Escape*. A letter of inquiry to the Stamford, Connecticut, blood bank records office got confirmation that the blood traces matched the types for the Monroes and Hamiltons.

Both couples were on record as generous donors. The letter of confirmation closed their files.

A YOUNG, WHITE-JACKETED WAITER on staff at the Queen Anne Yacht Club waited at the dock as the *Fancy Free* was tied up. He came aboard bearing on a silver tray an envelope addressed to Mr. Abner Chesterton. After receiving a generous tip and an order for drinks and lunch, the boy left.

"It's from The Consortium," Sir Abner said, opening the envelope. He looked at the letter. "Naturally it's in code. Pardon me." He went below to the captain's berth where he kept an encoding-decoding book.

By the time the deciphering was completed and Sir Abner had rejoined the others in the afterdeck salon, the luncheon was served.

Track took a sip of his double Seagram's Seven over ice. "It's not too hard to figure out. The missing boat has been found, right?"

"Absolutely, Dan, old son," Sir Abner said. "It had been converted for running dope. Naturally the Monroes and Hamiltons were not aboard. But their bloodstains were."

George Beegh looked out the door over the stern. He could see the open sea and the wide horizon. "The fish have already fed off those poor people." Before he could say more, a voice interrupted him.

"Ahoy, *Fancy Free!*"

Zulu could be heard on the side deck returning the greeting. "Ah, it's you, Commodore Durham-Jones. Please come aboard. The owner is in the salon."

"Uhail gani, Nahodha?" Durham-Jones inquired in Swahili.

"I am fine, thank you, sah," Zulu replied.

A moment later, the commodore joined Track, Sir Abner and Desiree. "Welcome back to the Queen Anne Yacht Club and a good afternoon to you all."

"Likewise," Track said.

Durham-Jones walked to Desiree and took her hand, kissing it lightly. "And did you enjoy your trip through the primitive islands hereabouts?"

"Very much," Desiree said demurely. "It was such a thrill."

"Indeed," Durham-Jones said. He turned to Sir Abner. "I say, Chesterton. Did you receive your telegram?"

"Yes, thank you. A bit of news from my broker."

"Good, I hope."

"Not really," Sir Abner said. "But it makes me the more determined because of it."

"Good show! British stiff upper lip and all that, what?"

George fell into his crewman's role. "May I fix you a drink, sir?"

"My usual gin and tonic, lad," Durham-Jones ordered. He waited for his drink before continuing. "I presume that since all went well, Old Arlo gave you good advice and directions."

"Yes," Track said. "We got a little tired of the sun and water, so we thought we'd come back for a while. Perhaps we'll do a little of the local nightlife."

"Then I shall be most presumptuous and remind you that the lovely Mrs. Hunter has already invited me to act as your guide," Durham-Jones said. "Here in Kingston we've some absolutely smashing nightclubs—dining, dancing and all that."

"We'll certainly give them a try," Track said. "But before we sample the more genteel forms of entertainment, I'd like to hit the bars along the dock."

"I say! That's rough going," Durham-Jones warned him.

"I'll be careful," Track said. "It's a hobby of mine. I like to mix with the riffraff."

"You'll certainly find them along the waterfront," Durham-Jones said. "All you have to do is go through the club's front gate and turn west. Within a few blocks you'll be in the heart of an area known locally as Robbers' Roost. Of course you've been there before. That's where Old Arlo lives."

"We didn't stop at any of the bars," Track said.

Durham-Jones laughed and pointed to Zulu, who was visible through the starboard porthole. "Of course if you have Captain Baharia with you, there shouldn't be too many difficulties."

"I'll have him and Seaman Big, as well," Track assured him.

"At any rate, I guarantee you an adventurous evening," Durham-Jones said. "But before you go, won't you be my guests at the club for an early supper?" He glanced at Desiree. "I would most certainly enjoy your company."

"Thank you," Track said.

Durham-Jones finished his drink and sat it down. "Jolly good then! I shall see you all at my table at sevenish, what?"

Desiree watched the Englishman depart, then turned and glared at Track. "So you are going to visit the seamy side of town, hey? And what am I supposed to do in the meantime? Sit here and twiddle my thumbs?"

"I had hoped you would enjoy spending an evening with me, my dear," Sir Abner said to Desiree. "Am I really such bad company?"

"Of course not, you old darling!" Desiree said. She walked over and embraced him. "I am so glad you're here." She looked at Track reproachfully. "If it weren't for you, this entire mission would be unbearable."

Track sighed and got up to pour some more Seagram's Seven. "I am not going to those places because I think barroom brawls are excellent forms of recreation, Desiree. It is a way to let a certain element of society know that we're still around and will be returning to the sea in a couple of days."

Desiree wasn't buying his line. "I can see the reluctance in your face," she said sarcastically. "What a sacrifice! I'm such an ungrateful bitch."

George came to his uncle's defense. "Jesus, Desiree! You don't think a bunch of cutthroat dope runners are hanging around the Queen Anne Yacht Club, do you?"

"I hope you both get your noses broken!" Desiree snapped. She turned and walked toward the door leading below decks. At that moment Zulu came in, and she glared at him furiously. "You too!"

With a puzzled expression, Zulu watched her disappear below.

"Jeez!" George said. "We sure as hell don't need air conditioning aboard. It's icy in here now."

Track grinned. "I think I'm looking forward to a nice hostile drinking crowd."

STUBBY BOUDREAUX SAT IN HIS USUAL PLACE, his chair tipped back as he viewed the small marina through half-closed eyes. He cast a lazy glance over at his nephew Marvin Leroy Firpo who sat up on the dock railing, staring at nothing with an expression as blank as his mind.

Stubby pulled out a pinch of Red Chief Chewing Tobacco and shoved it into his cheek, working it slowly and deliberately.

Marvin Leroy came to life. "Looky yonder."

"Where?" Stubby asked, feeling too comfortable and relaxed to expend even the small amount of energy it would take to turn his head.

"Yonder."

"Yonder, hell! Shithead, *yonder* could be anywheres," Stubby said. The flash of temper brought him to wakefulness and made him the angrier. He turned and glanced in the direction that Marvin Leroy was looking. His eyes opened wider and he tipped the chair forward, standing up. "Damnation! Howdy, Pedro."

Pedro Rojas, owner of the Cuban bar in Hobart, walked down the dock toward them. His automobile, a year-old BMW, was parked at the curb near the marina's edge. "I wan' talk wit' you, Stubby."

"Jesus Christ!" Stubby said. He glanced around carefully and opened the door leading to the interior of his small chandlery. "Hurry on inside."

Pedro went into the store. He turned to face his colleague. "I got some 'portant stuff to talk about, Stubby."

"I reckon you do," Stubby said in a worried tone. "You know we ain't supposed to be seen together."

Marvin Leroy came inside. "Howdy, Pedro."

Stubby whirled his fat carcass and faced his nephew. "Git the hell outta here, shithead. This don't concern you. Now git! *Git!*"

"Aw!" Marvin Leroy complained. But he quickly obeyed, leaving the two men alone.

Stubby was visibly agitated. "Goddamn it, Pedro. Yo're gonna git us both in big trouble."

Pedro held up his hands in a calming gesture. "I wouldn'a come if it wasn't ver' 'portant, Stubby. We got to get the guys a boat."

"Hell, I set 'em up with one—the *Fancy Free*," Stubby said. "Anyhow, they already had the other'n them two couples was on."

"The boat got used up, man," Pedro said. "Too many runs. So they sunk it. The others is used up, too. They got to have one."

Stubby gestured toward his marina. "Well, there ain't nothin' for 'em right now. What happened to the *Fancy Free*?"

"I don' know, man. They ain't got her yet, I guess," Pedro said. "Fact is, they lost one or somethin'."

"Looky here, Pedro, you tell them dumb bastards to git that *Fancy Free*," Stubby said. "It's a goddamn Gulfstar Motor Yacht, a damned good boat. Them folks took her to the same places that *Escape to Paradise* went. All they gotta do is look."

"Okay, I tell them, Stubby," Pedro said. "But you get 'nother boat quick."

"They ain't no more, goddamn it all to hell!" Stubby yelled. "It's the *Fancy Free* or nothin'." He pointed out at the marina. "Go out there and take a look around. If you see anymore goddamn boats that'd serve the purpose, you just let me know about it."

Pedro remained cool. "Lissen to me, Stubby. They wan' boats, you unnerstan'? If they don' get boats, then there's gonna be trouble."

Stubby snarled. "Don't you try no threat on me, goddamn you, Pedro!"

"Calmate," Pedro said. "There ain't no reason to be mad for me—I din't do something. I just pass the word, okay?" He walked to the door. "All I say is they need a boat. You say you don't got one. Okay. Then the guys will double up and really go after that *Fancy Free*—if she be on the Spanish Main, they find her." He scowled a farewell and left.

Marvin Leroy walked through the door. "What'd ol' Pedro want, Uncle Stubby?"

"Never you mind, shithead," Stubby barked. Then he calmed down and slowly shook his head. "I'm sure glad I ain't sailin' on that poor fuckin' *Fancy Free*!"

IT WAS QUIET IN THE AFTERDECK SALON. Desiree, listening to the music from a radio turned down low, looked pensively out over the harbor of the Queen Anne Yacht Club.

Sir Abner's attention was being absorbed by the book he was reading and the delicious taste of the Cubana Real tobacco in the bowl of his pipe. After a while he glanced up and noticed his beautiful companion's sad expression. He spoke softly. "Lost in a reverie, my dear?"

Desiree smiled sadly. "Yes, old darling."

Sir Abner laid aside his book. He stood up and walked over to join her on the settee. "Care to share any of it with a tried and true friend?"

The lovely young woman sighed. "I was once completely in charge of my life," she said. "I asked nothing from no one. Everything I needed I provided for myself, and there was no fear or hesitation about anything I chose to do. I ran guns as good as any man—"

The older man puffed on his pipe. "Then you met Mr. Dan Track."

"He has torn a hole in my heart—in my soul!" Desiree said. "I want to continue my life as it has always been, yet at the same time I want to change. I don't know what to do."

"You are in love," Sir Abner said.

"Of course," Desiree said. "I admit that—I accept it. But I cannot handle it. Sometimes I feel as if I am not really a woman."

"Nonsense, my dear," Sir Abner said with a light laugh. "You are, most certainly, a woman—and a beautiful one at that."

She smiled at the compliment. "I should be happy, *non*? The man I love also loves me. We should both be delirious, but we're not. In fact, we are practically at each other's throat."

"Dan is a sensitive fellow, believe me, Desiree," Sir Abner assured her.

"Sensitive!" she exclaimed angrily. "I am here suffering. And where is he? Out having a good time with the 'boys'—that's where!"

"This evening's outing is work," Sir Abner reminded her. "I'm sure if the two of you simply bare what is in your hearts, this conflict will end."

Hope lit up her eyes. "Do you really think so, Sir Abner?"

"Of course, Desiree, dear," he said. "Beneath that exterior is a caring man. I believe the Hispanics have a word for it—*simpàtico*. It's difficult to translate, but it means one who is tuned in to others' feelings, someone who can read the vibrations in the air about him, someone who—"

The sound of happy, singing masculine voices broke into the conversations as Track, Zulu and George burst into the salon.

Track, a little drunk, had a bloody nose and a blackened eye. His shirt collar was torn and his trousers were filthy. "You should've been there!" he whooped. "We cleaned the fuckin' bar out."

Zulu and George, in as bad shape, joined in the laughter.

Track, giggling, went over and collapsed on the settee opposite Desiree and Sir Abner. "We even sent a coupla cops to the hospital. God Almighty! What a fight! The best goddamn brawl I've ever been in!" He grinned wickedly. "And I needed it, brother."

Desiree glared at him, then leaped to her feet and stalked out of the salon.

"What the hell's the matter with her?" Track asked his sodden buddies. "We won, didn't we?"

8

The sun was a white-hot disk in the pale, cloudless sky. It blazed down pitilessly on a mirror-still Caribbean, while not a hint of breeze offered any cooling relief.

Track, standing on the flying bridge with Zulu, wiped at the sweat that seeped from under the bandanna he had wrapped around his head. He'd pulled on a long-sleeved T-shirt to avoid a bad sunburn in the cruel heat that baked the yacht.

The swelling in Track's eye had gone down quite a bit, but his jaw was still sore from the fight in the bar. He winced again under the slamming rays of the sun. The small American flag on the stern hung listlessly from its staff in the still air. "This weather pattern was hell on old-time seamen who depended on wind power to drive their vessels."

"Ah, yes, Major," Zulu said. "It is called the doldrums. A situation marked by dead calms and weak fluctuating winds. Those old sailor men would be becalmed, standing motionless in this scorching hell. I have read that many ships spent weeks barely moving while facing the double danger of running out of food and water—not to mention heat stroke or madness from despair."

Track pointed down to the open hatches over the twin diesel engines where George Beegh was pretending to be working. "If this breakdown was for real, we'd be in the same condition."

"Actually, we would be even worse off," Zulu pointed out. "We have no sails. If a fresh wind were to smarten up, we'd not be able to take advantage of it with disabled engines. Those seamen of bygone days would put out every square inch of canvas they carried and catch enough breeze to move them out of the doldrums, no matter how slowly."

Track sighed and took another wipe at the perspiration on his forehead. The *Fancy Free* had been simulating a mechanical failure for more than six hours. A recorded SOS message was periodically broadcast by their radio. But so far, there had been no response—particularly from the pirates they hoped to attract.

The inactivity was a sort of blessing to Track, George and Zulu. They needed a bit of rest to recuperate from the sojourn into the Robbers' Roost section of the Kingston waterfront. George, like his companions, had suffered minor injuries in the altercation in the waterfront saloon two nights before.

They had strolled into the Robbers' Roost and, acting like boorish, monied tourists, they had done their best to attract attention.

The first bar, not too far into the area, was large but rather quiet. Their entrance garnered only a couple of casual glances before the drinkers turned back to their beer and resumed their muted conversations.

The three took advantage of the situation to talk a bit loudly of their plans for the next day. Track had set things rolling with a casual but easily heard remark about where he wanted to go. "Those little islands south of the Pedro Cays are what intrigue me."

Zulu joined in. "Is dat where you wish to go, sah?"

"Certainly," Track said in the role of owner. "How much time do you figure it'll take us to get there, Captain Baharia?"

"No more den t'ree or four hours," Zulu said. "But you 'member, sah, dat is long way from anybody."

Track took a swig of his drink. "So what? The idea of this voyage was to get away, wasn't it?"

George took his cue. "We've been having trouble with that port engine, sir. There's a good chance it might give out on us."

Track took a swig of his beer. "Then, by God, we'll make do on the starboard engine, won't we?"

"Ver' risky, sah," Zulu seemed to caution him. "We be stuck out dere, nobody aroun' to help."

They spent an hour in the place. By that time they were convinced that no one there gave a damn about them, their trip or their boat. So they finished a final round of drinks and left the bar.

The next saloon was six blocks away—and most definitely not as friendly. Their entrance was greeted with outright dirty looks. One man, drunk beyond good sense, rose from his table and staggered toward them on some menacing errand concocted in his intoxicated mind. Zulu put his big hand on the guy's face and shoved him back so hard that he hit the wall a dozen feet away and careened off onto a table.

Three seafaring black men who had been sitting there picked him up and tossed him aside to collapse on the floor. One of the trio, a dangerous-looking sort with a large earring, glared at Zulu. "Careful dere, bruddah. You come close to spill my beer."

Zulu grinned. "Den I would buy you one for to replace it, bruddah."

"Damn right you buy one for to replace it," the sailor replied, glaring. Then he sat down and rejoined his two friends in whatever subject they had been discussing.

Track, Zulu and George repeated their staged conversation, but drew only casual interest. None of the bar patrons, they decided, could have cared less about where they were going or the condition of their engines.

It was time to move on.

The last place they found was called the Blue Lantern. Track looked around and could not see any type of lantern—blue or otherwise. Only the weak glow of bare sixty-watt bulbs lit the dismal bar.

Track and Company walked in a bit unsteadily, simulating a few hours of heavy drinking. They went to the bar and Zulu banged on the top.

"Barman, bring us Guinness. We t'ree fellahs got a big t'irst."

"You bet!" George said loudly. "We gotta lubricate ourselves for a week off the Pedro Cays, baby." He simulated drunken laughter. "'Specially since the damn engines ain't gonna get us back."

"Sure they will," Track said, throwing an arm around the other's shoulder. "Y'know why?"

"No," George said, shaking his head unsteadily. "You tell me why."

"'Cause you're the best damn engineman that ever sailed the whole goddamned Spanish Main!" Track said, laughing loudly.

"Aw!" George said modestly. "You're only saying that 'cause it's true!"

They dissolved into laughter, but a cold voice from the other end of the bar cut into their merriment. "You fellahs come to slum wit' us poor people?"

Track looked up and stared into the cold gaze of Old Arlo's nephew Harry. He squinted and shook his head. "Do I know you?"

"Sure," Harry said. "You cheated my po' ol' uncle for a map and a charted course. You're a stingy rich mon."

Track smiled. "Fuck you."

Harry stepped away from the bar. "I don't lak you big mouth, 'mrican rich mon."

Track moved slowly out onto the floor, tensed and ready. "Then—as they say in Dixie—hush my mouth."

Harry wasted no time in getting things under way. He sprang forward, throwing a hard right cross. The three men with him joined in the attack, colliding bodily with Track and Company. No weapons were used; fists and feet flew freely as the melee developed.

From that point on, international relations went rapidly downhill.

Everyone in the bar joined in. It was to the patrons' credit that they didn't all gang up on the strangers. A few grudges between them leaped back to life as a small riot developed.

Track happily punched Harry until the black man spun off into a swarm of brawlers. He didn't see Old Arlo's nephew again—and didn't give him much thought, either. He was too damned busy throwing punches and ducking others while teaming up with Zulu and George to form a small protective circle to keep their personal injuries to a minimum.

Then the police showed up. These enforcers of the law showed as much enthusiasm for brawling as did the crowd, and a few of them ended up unconscious on the sawdust-strewn floor before mass arrests began.

By then Track, Zulu and George had slammed their way to the door. When they reached the street, they caught sight of Harry. Bleeding from the nose, the Jamaican stood with his friends, but he made no move toward Track and Company. He merely pointed at them.

"I see you later—you can count on dat!" Then he and his small gang disappeared up an alley.

Track and his friends headed back for the more sedate environs of the Queen Anne Yacht Club.

Now, rubbing an aching head, Track sat on the flying bridge. He glanced over at Zulu. "What do you make of Old Arlo's nephew?" he asked.

"Harry?" Zulu shrugged. "A very unpleasant chap. Not to be trusted."

"My opinion, too," Track said. "But one thing about the guy really puzzles me. He didn't use a knife or any other weapon in that fight we had with him and his buddies."

"Most unusual, I agree, Major," Zulu said. "Perhaps he didn't want to face serious charges from the law."

"Maybe he didn't want to stop us from taking the *Fancy Free* to sea," Track mused.

"A good point, Major," Zulu remarked. "He may well be part of the pirate gang."

Desiree suddenly appeared from the lower deck. "Sir Abner says there's a blip on the radar."

"Right," Track said. He shouted down to George. "Look busy! Company's coming!"

"Right," George said. He grabbed a wrench and leaned over the engine.

Zulu scanned the horizon with his binoculars. After a few moments he pointed to the west. "There she is, Major. A small craft approaching off the starboard bow."

Track used his own field glasses, focusing on the approaching vessel. "Could well be more of the bastards." He walked to the open hatch of the afterdeck salon. "Are you ready down there?"

"Right you are, Dan, old son," Sir Abner called back. "Desiree and I are primed for action."

Track yelled at George. "How about you, kid?"

"Aye, aye, sir," George replied. He lifted the PZF44 rocket launcher then restowed it out of sight in the engine hold. "I've got six rounds down here. Even if they show up in a goddamned battle cruiser, I'll sink the bastards."

Track pointed out to the west. "It's hardly a cruiser. But if it's who we think it is, sink it, anyway."

The approaching vessel grew close enough for Zulu to identify its type. "It appears to be a small fishing boat, Major."

"We'll see," Track said.

A half hour later, a battered old boat with a loud, chugging engine drew alongside. A black man wearing a broad-brimmed straw hat that was in as bad condition as the little ship leaned from the pilot house. "Ahoy, *Fancy Free*. We be hearin' your SOS. Mebbe you lak a tow outta ol' doldrums, eh?"

Crouching behind the settee in the salon, Sir Abner with his Sterling submachine gun and Desiree, holding an Uzi, were ready to spray the visitor with swarms of 9 mm slugs.

Track could see that there was only one other man aboard. All evidence pointed to the visitors being honest fishermen who had gone out of their way to answer the SOS.

Track gave the "all clear" signal to George by removing the bandanna and wiping his neck with it.

George suddenly stood up and waved his wrench. "I've got it, Cap'n," he hollered at Zulu. "We'll be under way in another fifteen minutes."

Zulu nodded to him then smiled at the fisherman. "We are all right, bruddah. T'ank you for lookin' in on us."

"You be mos' welcome, Cap'n," the fisherman said with a grin. "We got to help each ot'er out heah. So long and good luck."

Track walked to the rail and tossed a fat roll of American dollars onto the fishing boat's deck. "That's for your trouble."

The fisherman's companion, a young man, scrambled for the money. He showed it to the other, then turned and waved. "T'ank you, sah. T'ank you so much!"

Track and Zulu watched the fishermen depart, their chugging engine's sound diminishing as they drew farther away. Track looked at his companion. "People like that renew my faith in human nature."

"Yes indeed, Major," Zulu agreed. "Unfortunately, we've gotten so accustomed to seeing evil in our fellow creatures that we rarely look for good."

Track sighed. "You could be right, but remember, we can't afford to let up for an instant." Suddenly his eyes widened. "Wait a minute—wait one goddamned minute!"

"What's the matter, Major?"

"What in the hell would a poor fisherman be doing with radio equipment in a beat-up old vessel like—"

"Blip off the port stern!" Sir Abner called from below. "Approaching fast."

"That no good son of a bitch was checking up on us!" Track exclaimed. "Those concerned citizens were doing recon duty for another vessel—an armed one!"

Zulu pulled his Webley revolver and spun the cylinder. "So much for kindly thoughts about our fellow man, Major."

"Yeah!" He turned to the stern. "George?"

"I heard," George replied grimly. "Bring on the sons of bitches!"

They heard the angry snarl of an approaching high-speed cabin cruiser. It closed on the *Fancy Free* in a matter of a few minutes.

It eased up alongside, the engines' maintaining minimal speed. There were only two men on the flying bridge, but Track was willing to give odds that there were more behind the curtained portholes of the main cabin.

The pilot of the craft waved and displayed a gold-toothed grin. He was a swarthy Hispanic, with tightly curled hair. "Howdy, amigo, we heard your SOS—you need help, no?"

Track walked up to the rail of his own flying bridge. A piece of canvas hanging over the rail concealed the Franchi SPAS-12 shotgun he carried. "We have a little engine trouble," he said.

"I'm a *mecánico experto*, man," the pilot said. "So is my frien' here."

His companion, a black man about the size of Zulu, leered and waved. "I fix him up good, m'sieur—no problem."

"In fac'", the pilot said, laughing, "*todos mis amigos*—all my frien's—fix him up good." He suddenly shouted. "*¡Vamonos, muchachos!*"

Track tightened his grip on the SPAS-12 and brought it up fast. He held down the trigger and blew the two men on the flying bridge off their boat into the water on the other side.

Sir Abner and Desiree barely had time to kick out a couple of short fire bursts each before the pirate craft's engines roared to life and it veered off quickly, putting space between it and the *Fancy Free*.

"Jesus!" Track said with a touch of admiration in his voice. "Talk about contingencies!"

"Right, Major," Zulu agreed. "They had a man at the controls in the main cabin in case of trouble." He watched the enemy boat make a wide turn. "They are positioning themselves."

"We're in for a running sea fight," Track said.

"In that case," Zulu said calmly. "I suggest we man our own battle stations."

Track turned to yell at George, but the energetic young man had already slammed the engine hatches shut and was heading for the forepeak, lugging the launcher and ammunition with him. George glanced up just before he disappeared into the afterdeck salon. "Batten down the hatches!" he yelled happily.

Track and Zulu joined the others below.

Sir Abner's battle station was at the control console below decks. His job, as usual, was to act as combat helmsman.

Desiree would stay in the salon with Zulu. George, of course, manned his rockets up forward, while Track would go wherever he was needed—or had the best opportunity to inflict the most damage.

The Gulfstar's engines kicked over, and Sir Abner pressed forward on the throttles, revving up to the proper rpm before throwing in the clutches. The motor yacht shuddered, then leaped forward, throwing out a wide wake.

Another sea battle was on in the Caribbean.

9

George Beegh was having trouble drawing a good bead on the pirate craft. The *Fancy Free*'s bow continually jumped up then slapped itself down on the ocean as the chase developed. The rocket launcher's sight danced at crazy angles in front of his face.

Track remained on the flying bridge directing Sir Abner from his vantage point. "I want to get in close enough to give George a shot at the bastard," he yelled. "And we'll have to slow down to make the boat a steady firing platform."

"This is proving a bit more difficult than our former encounter," Sir Abner shouted back. "That's an Intercantieri boat the blighter is piloting out there. He's a hell of a lot more maneuverable and faster than the first bastard we took on."

"We'll have to work this thing like coordination between a quarterback and a wide receiver," Track said. "Work the angles, Sir Abner. Think NFL."

"NFL?" Sir Abner inquired. "What in the deuce is that? If I work any angles, I shall do as it is done in the Rugby Football Union."

Track laughed. "I didn't know there were any 'angles' in rugby."

"Ignorant colonial!" Sir Abner snapped. "You've never seen the beauty of running dropkick over the crossbars, have you?"

"I'm afraid not," Track admitted.

"Then not to worry, old son," Sir Abner said. "As a former Rugby Union leftwing three-quarter, I bloody well know my 'angles'!"

Sir Abner doubled his concentration on the fleeing pirate, trying to get into the man's head to figure out his next move. The Englishman veered to port, but the quarry maintained a straight course.

"Oh, rot!" Sir Abner shouted in anger at the sudden increase of distance between them. He attempted more throttle, but both engines were going full bore.

"Fuck it!" Track yelled. "George, shoot at the bastard!"

George wasted no time in squeezing off a round. The rear of the launcher was not positioned properly, however, and the backblast blew off the foredeck railing, sending the twisted metal rods spinning out into the broad expanse of ocean. The rocket he fired did no more than streak high and wide.

George glanced at the damage he'd done their own craft. "Oh, shit! I might've sunk *us*!"

"Just be careful," Track cautioned him. "Remember that you're just as dangerous rearward for a short distance as you are to the front."

Suddenly Sir Abner yelled. "I've got the blighter!" He had pulled another port turn while the pirate had swung starboard. This instantly closed them up nearly twenty-five yards.

Track saw the opportunity to once again use the SPAS-12. He cradled it in his arms, ready to bring the shotgun up for some quick shots, but suddenly the windshield on the flying bridge flew apart and chunks of decking were flung up around him.

"The bastard's got a heavy machine gun!" George yelled up at his uncle.

"No shit!" Track said.

Another row of spaced shots tore into the flying bridge, forcing Track to roll aft and drop down onto the after-deck.

At the same time George cut loose again with the PZF44.

The rocket went in low and hit the water. Owing to the unusually flat trajectory, the projectile's explosive nose missed the water and it bounced back up and streaked in low at the bow of the pirate boat. It hit the target, but the angle of the strike caused the brunt of the resulting explosion to roar outward away from the boat.

But enough of the blast went down and inward to take off one of the rudders. Now the pirate's maneuverability was seriously restricted.

"Look at the bastard!" George yelled, not really aware of the damage he'd caused. "He's making wide turns."

"Good show, lad!" Sir Abner said. "I believe you've somehow damaged his steering mechanism."

Track had retaken his position on the flying bridge. He pointed. "There's the machine gun—a Browning .50! See the muzzle out of the rear window by the cockpit?"

"Yeah!" George yelled. "Sir Abner, get me a shot there!"

"Right-o, lad!" Sir Abner hollered. "Here we go, then!"

The *Fancy Free* was no longer pressed to maintain full speed. She pulled back and made a wide circle, easily maintaining contact with the damaged vessel. The pirates showed their frustration by firing long-range bursts of .50-caliber bullets that splashed the water and sang through the air above Track and Company.

"I say, George," Sir Abner addressed him loudly, "are you ready?"

"Is the Pope Catholic?" George rejoined.

Sir Abner hesitated. "Well—yes, he is, most certainly. But what has that—"

"He means yes," Track said.

"Then why not say so!" Sir Abner said testily. He again pushed against the throttles, and the *Fancy Free* began a rocket run.

The incoming machine-gun fire increased in ferocity as the distance closed between the two vessels. George, his eye pressed hard against the sight, ignored the whine and slap of the heavy slugs around him as he focused all his concentration on one thing—hitting the son of a bitch out there ahead of him.

Track grimaced and ducked from the growing fusillade that began to make serious hits onto the motor yacht. *Do it right, George,* he beseeched his nephew in his mind, *don't let us get blown to hell for nothing!*

The *Fancy Free* drew so close that Track and Company could make out the facial features of the pirates.

"I say, George," Sir Abner said in an amazingly calm voice, "are you going to shoot the bugger with that thing or beat him over the head with it?"

George responded to the question by pulling the trigger.

A belch, a roar of backblast and the ignition of the rocket all sounded simultaneously. The small 81 mm missile zipped out of the tube and crossed the small expanse of water to fly just across the pirates' gunwale and slap into the back of the cabin.

The explosion nearly capsized the craft, but it was to the credit of the Intercantieri boat builders that she not only righted herself but continued forward.

"Veer off!" Track warned as the machine gunfire resumed. Despite Sir Abner's evasive maneuvering, Track was again forced off the flying bridge. He unceremoniously slid down the ladder and dived into the afterdeck salon to take cover behind the reinforced settee.

Zulu and Desiree, each tightly gripping their Uzis, were already crouched there. Zulu grinned. "How are we doing, Major?"

Track realized that the big black man and Desiree had been completely unaware of the progress of the battle from their combat stations. "George has made two hits on the son of a bitch," Track said, bringing them up to date. "He's done some kind of damage to their rudders or steering cables, so we're able to outmaneuver them."

Desiree's eyes were alight with the lust for battle. "Then let us close in and destroy him!"

"That, my darling," Track said, "is an excellent idea." He crawled forward, then had to slam himself flat on the deck as the starboard windows of the salon disintegrated under two rapid firebursts from the heavy machine gun.

"Sir Abner," Track called, "we want to board her. Can you close in on her now?"

"Is the Archbishop of Canterbury from the Church of England?" Sir Abner crowed. "Tallyho!"

Track quickly leaped up and ran forward to the fore-peak. "George, we're going in for the kill. Throw out enough shit to make 'em get their heads down!"

"Will you act as my loader?" George asked.

"You got it, buddy." Track pulled a rocket from the rack and shoved it into the tube. He tapped George on the shoulder. "Get 'em, tiger!"

George raised up, swung the rear of the tube away from the cabin and pulled the trigger activating the magneto. As soon as the weapon fired, he ducked back down for another assist from his uncle.

They had time to get off four rounds before scrambling to the deck. Desiree and Zulu ran from the salon and joined them on the foredeck just as Sir Abner cut the engines.

Track wasted no time in leaping across the expanse between the two vessels, landing in the cockpit.

A quick glance inside the cabin showed a twisted machine-gun mount. It was a tribute to the gunner's strength and guts that he was still in a fighting mood after having his weapon literally blown out of his hands by one of George's rockets.

Crazed with fear and anger, he charged through the opening left by the explosion and leaped at Track, swinging a long, wicked boat hook.

Track raised the SPAS-12 and took the brunt of the blow across the receiver. His hands stung from the force of it. He twisted and delivered a horizontal buttstroke that collided heavily with the man's jaw, knocking him into the gunwale.

Another pirate leaped at Track, shoving a .45 Colt Commander into his face. He fired two wild shots in the split second it took Track to swing the muzzle of his shotgun around.

Track's trigger finger flexed but once. The blast of buckshot hit the pistolero with the force of a battering ram, slamming him through the doorway, across the cabin and into the control console.

By then both Zulu and Desiree were behind Track in the cockpit, but there was no room for them to effectively use their Uzi submachine guns.

George, as arranged, stood on the side deck of the *Fancy Free*, in a covering stance. He was ready to employ the new model AR-15 9 mm that he deftly held in his eager hands.

Track stepped back and nodded to Zulu. The big man pulled the concussion grenade from the pouch on his pistol belt. After quickly removing the pin, he tossed the grenade inside the cabin. It bounced once, then went down the ladder below decks.

An explosion shook the boat, and debris and dust blew up through the door. Track slipped to the top of the ladder in time to see a dazed man, his ears and nose bleeding, stumbling up toward him.

"Hold it, asshole," Track said in a matter-of-fact tone, "or I'll blow your fucking head back down below."

The pirate, confused as hell by concussion, could still raise the Obregon .45 automatic in his hand. He aimed it at Track.

So Track kept his word and blew his fucking head back down below.

The man's body hit the deck. An instant later Track leaped down and landed on top of him. Without time for a leisurely look around, Track pumped off three quick shots—two solid slugs and one load of buckshot—that ripped open mattresses on the bunk and blew in the door of the head located in the forepeak.

The man who'd been hiding there stepped out, his eyes wide in shock. The front of his body had been ripped open by the shotgun blasts and splinters from the door. He managed to take one step before pitching headfirst to the deck.

Zulu and Desiree came in after Track and quickly searched the remainder of the boat. Desiree was disappointed. "Everyone that was aboard is dead."

"We really should have gotten prisoners," Zulu said.

"We still can," Track said. "Remember that cheap little fishing boat that played the Good Samaritan with us?"

"Ah!" Desiree said happily remembering.

"Shall we go, then?" Zulu asked.

"That's the best suggestion I've heard all day," Track said. He led them back topside, and all three jumped back aboard the *Fancy Free*.

Sir Abner was at the control console located in the shot-up flying bridge. "What now, Dan?"

"We'll run down those phony fisherman that fingered us for these guys," Track said. He held up a cautioning hand to George. "No rockets this time, big guy. We're after prisoners."

George pointed to the disabled pirate boat. "Are we going to sink this one first?"

"Nope," Track said. "I want these bastards to be found. If I know my dope runner, he'll take this one as a personal challenge."

"Yeah," George said in agreement. He looked at the dead men and the boat that was shot up so badly that it listed at a crazy angle. "This should be enough to piss 'em off."

"Full spccd ahead, Sir Abner," Track said. "Let's get that other bastard." He nodded to George. "Stand the radar watch, if you please, Mister Beegh."

"Aye, aye, sir!"

The *Fancy Free*, a bit worse for wear but still able to fight and sail, bit her bow into the Caribbean and pushed her way rapidly across the Spanish Main while George Beegh kept his eye on the radar screen.

It took less than an hour to pick out the slowly moving boat from among the stationary blips of islands. George kept Sir Abner on course as the *Fancy Free*'s two diesels kept the screws turning at the designated rpm.

Zulu caught sight of the fugitives first. "Off the port bow!" he shouted.

Track looked through his binoculars, straining his eyes until he was sure. "That's them all right. I recognize that big straw hat."

The phony fisherman hove to and waited for the other boat to draw up on him. He stepped out of the cabin and waved. "Ahoy, *Fancy Free*."

"Ahoy, *Grass*," Track responded.

"We are not the *Grass*, mon," the "fisherman" said. "The name o' dis boat be de *Mary O*."

"No, it isn't," Track said. "The name of that tub is the *Grass*, and we're the *Lawn Mower*." He raised the SPAS-12.

"Oh, shit!" the man said. He suddenly dropped to the deck and his partner leaped into the door of the cabin, wielding a Kashmirov assault rifle.

Track's load of buckshot blew him overboard into the ocean.

George kicked off three rounds with the 9 mm AR-15. The impact of the rounds on the other pirate's body made him twitch violently as he dropped the Browning auto he'd pulled from his shirt.

George looked at his rifle, then glanced at Track. "Y'know," he said, "I'm beginning to grow real fond of this baby."

"It didn't leave much behind in the way of prisoners, though," Track remarked.

George shrugged. "It was a case of 'do or die.'"

Track nodded. "Literally."

10

Track, with Zulu and Sir Abner following, walked slowly around the starboard side deck of the *Fancy Free*, assessing the damage. Desiree, standing watch on the flying bridge, idly listened to their conversation as she scanned the ocean for any unwelcome visitors.

"Our sturdy ship took her share of hits," Track said. He stuck his finger into a deep hole just above the foredeck. Then he pointed up to the empty frame where the windshield had been around the flying bridge. He grinned at Desiree. "Is it breezy up there?"

Desiree only smiled a little and winked at him, then went back to her guard duty.

"We're still in good mechanical condition, however," Sir Abner pointed out, "and we can bloody well continue to hold our own."

Zulu shook his head in polite disagreement. "I fear we've gone a bit low on the ammunition, Sir Abner. Without a resupply, we're not quite up to snuff."

Desiree swept the horizon through Track's powerful binoculars. "It is quiet enough out there," she announced. "Perhaps this is a good time to make a replenishment run to shore."

"I agree," Track said. "We're in a good defense posture, but we could hardly press on like we have been doing. I'll set a course for the Queen Anne Yacht Club."

"I don't think we can do that, old son," Sir Abner said. "The Consortium's influence was great enough to allow us into Jamaica without a customs check. However, even their weighty pull won't extend to an obviously shot-up vessel. The authorities would be forced to investigate."

Zulu nodded his agreement. "Quite right, Sir Abner. And the press would most certainly make an appearance, as well."

"Publicity is the last thing The Consortium desires," Sir Abner said. "Any undue notoriety would greatly reduce the organization's ability to look after its interests."

George Beegh rested on the afterdeck listening to the conversation. "We need bullets," he said, breaking the situation down into the simplest of terms. "How do we get them?"

"Through The Consortium, of course," Sir Abner said. "But the ammunition will have to be brought out to us via seaplane. That includes our food and fresh water, too."

"Okay," Track said. "That's even better. Come into the salon with me. I have a great idea."

Sir Abner, Zulu and George stepped inside after him. They stood silently waiting while Track walked slowly around the compartment in deep thought.

Suddenly he took a deep breath and exploded into a karate *mae geri* front kick that sent the top of the dining table flying from its center post. The heavy piece of wood spun over three times before crashing to the deck.

"What the hell did you do that for?" George asked.

Track didn't answer. Instead he aimed a *mawashi geri* side kick at the center post. The heavy four-by-four broke off and flew into the window, crashing through it. Splintered glass scattered over the side deck.

Desiree's disturbed voice came down from the flying bridge. "What is going on in there?"

Sir Abner leaned through the freshly made opening in the window. "Not to worry, my dear. Dan is simply practicing his karate." He pulled his head back inside and faced Track. "Would you be kind enough to explain your insanity?"

"Don't worry about the glass," Track said. "It would have been removed, anyway."

Zulu was puzzled. "What in the world for, Major?"

"For the machine gun."

"What machine gun?" George asked.

"The heavy job that The Consortium is going to fly out to us," Track said with a wide grin. "Weren't you impressed with the damage the pirate did with that Browning?"

"Yeah!" George said happily. "You want to mount it where the table is, er, *was*, right?"

"Right," Track said. "Since we no longer have to make any pretences about the *Fancy Free* being a peaceful pleasure craft, we can set this afterdeck salon up as a machine gun station."

"Jolly good!" Sir Abner said. He glanced around the compartment. "I say! It shall be exactly as in the bomber planes of World War II. Only in this case, the gunner will be able to fire to both sides and the rear, too."

"We can use a combination of armor piercing and tracers," Track said. "That way we can be sure of being able to both punch inside and start fires, as well. And the tracers help in aiming by letting the gunner track where his bursts go."

"I suggest we make up a list of our wants immediately," Sir Abner said. "I can encode them and radio The Consortium contact in Kingston."

"I've been meaning to ask you," Track said, "who is our contact there?"

"I must admit with a great deal of embarrassment that I've absolutely no idea," Sir Abner said.

Zulu was thoughtful. "Could it be our friend Commodore Durham-Jones?"

"Possibly," Sir Abner said. "All I know is that we broadcast in code on a certain frequency, and the man—whoever he is—will pick up the message and take appropriate action."

Desiree, still on watch, had grown tired of listening to them. She shouted down at her companions. "A little less talk and more action, *s'il vous plaît*! This empty sea around us will not remain that way long."

PHILIPPE MATAMORE SAT IN THE BOW of the launch as its small battery-driven motor carried him toward the landing beach on Ile-a-Salut.

He had been to Port-au-Prince for a few days to visit his Aunt Charmine. The poor lady, after years of working both the streets and a back alley crib, had been going downhill fast of late. Now that she was nearing sixty, her early life-style was taking its toll. The latest medical assault on her, which had included a hysterectomy, had left her depressed and without energy.

Matamore hadn't seen her in nearly a year, and the change in her disturbed him greatly. He could still recall his aunt as a pretty young woman, lustily taking on the men that he and his father brought to her.

His thoughts of Aunt Charmine quickly disappeared when he caught sight of who awaited him on the landing beach. Rather than his paramour Madeleine, it was the radio operator.

"*Plus vite!*" he said to the coxswain as he urged him to greater speed. There was something afoot that obviously needed his attention.

Five minutes later the launch rode in on the gentle swells and slid onto the white sand. Matamore jumped over the bow and hurried to the radioman. "*¿Qué paso?*" he asked in Spanish.

"*Hay problemas grandes,*" the man answered, handing him a slip of paper. "I wrote the messages down as they came in, *jefe.*"

Matamore quickly scanned the written lines:

1405 hours. Humberto has made contact with *Fancy Free*. They seem to be having problems with the engines. Humberto has withdrawn. Am moving in.
Henri

1420 hours. Have attacked *Fancy Free*. Big surprise. Heavily armed, but can do the job.
Henri

1445 hours. Am waiting for word from Henri.
Humberto.

1505 hours. *Fancy Free* coming up on the stern.
Humberto.

1511 hours. Our boys not aboard. Something amiss.
Humberto

1513 hours. We are under attack by *Fancy Free*.
Humberto.

Matamore read the last line. He looked at the radioman. "This is the final transmission?"

"*Sí, jefe.*" His voice was almost apologetic.

"This means that this *Fancy Free* has sunk three of our boats," Matamore said incredulously.

"*Perdóneme*, two," the radioman corrected him. "Henri's boat was found with his corpse and several of the dead crew still aboard. It was almost as if it were left there as a challenge."

"Get back to the communications shack and stay there," Matamore ordered. "If you hear anything, contact me immediately. I will be in my quarters."

"As you wish, *mi jefe*!" the man said, hurrying off.

Now lost deep in troubled thought, Matamore strode rapidly and angrily through the village toward the old plantation house at the top of the hill. He scarcely acknowledged the respectful greetings he received as he ascended the steep terrain in long, purposeful strides.

Madeleine Noire was waiting for him on the veranda as he arrived at the steps. The smile for her lover quickly faded from her face as she saw how troubled he was. She greeted him with a quick hug and a peck on the mouth.

"How was your trip, *chéri*?" she asked, worried.

"Fine," Matamore answered. "I must think. A situation has developed during my absence that requires a great deal of attention."

"Of course, *mon amour*." She slipped her arm through his and ascended the steps, allowing him to lead her through the house to the room he used for an office. Madeleine broke away from him and hurried to the refrigerator. She withdrew one of the many mugs in the freezer and poured it full of Miragoane beer. Then the woman hurried to the veranda and handed him the cold brew.

Matamore, pondering what seemed to be a declaration of war, took several sips before he spoke. "We have lost two excellent boats and recovered one badly damaged. There have also been several good men killed," he said softly. "The vessel we found seems to have been left for us as an insult and challenge."

"*Quelle domage!*" Madeline clucked in sympathy.

"The source of this trouble is a single vessel—the *Fancy Free*," Matamore said, beginning to pace. "It was first reported to be owned by rich Americans on a vacation. But evidently that is not so."

"What do you think is the truth of the matter?" Madeleine asked. She sat down in an oversize wicker chair. She knew that, in this mood, Matamore would engage her—and himself—in pensive conversation while he figured out the latest situation.

"Perhaps the United States Customs is springing a trap on us," Matamore said. He shrugged. "There is no doubt that if the legal restraints on them were removed, those agents could close down all drug smuggling operations in a matter of only a few weeks."

"Ah! The bastards!" Madelcine exclaimed angrily.

Matamore shook his head. *"Mais non,"* he said after a few moments of silent thought. "It could not be them. Why would they send out but one boat for such a mission?"

"You are right, of course," Madeleine said.

Matamore finished his beer. Madeleine took the mug away, then returned with a fresh frosted one filled up with more of the Haitian brew. He took it absentmindedly. "I think this is an act of revenge for some strange reason. A rival gang is challenging us—" He took a slow sip, then his eyes widened. *"Mais oui!* That is it!" He set the unfinished beer down on the veranda railing and hurried into his office.

Worried, Madeleine went after him. "Philippe! Philippe! What are you going to do?"

Matamore picked up the telephone on his desk. "I am going to gather all our resources, weapons, men and the fastest boats we can get our hands on."

Madeleine nervously wet her lips. "What will happen, *mon amour*?"

Philippe Matamore spoke through angrily clenched teeth. "I am going to gather enough good men and boats to destroy those bastards on the *Fancy Free*!"

TRACK AWOKE SLOWLY, stretching languidly. The lower deck cabin was dark, and he could hear the even, heavy breathing of three sleeping men—Zulu, Sir Abner and George.

He looked at the dull glow of the luminous dial of his Rolex Sea Dweller watch—it showed the hour to be three. His mind clicked further awake as he remembered that Desiree had the 2:00 to 4:00 A.M. watch. He swung out of the bunk and dropped lightly to the floor, tiptoeing barefoot across the deck to the ladder leading topside.

The moon was full, reflecting brightly in the gentle swells of the Caribbean as Track stepped out of the salon onto the side deck. "Desiree," he called softly.

"Yes?" She walked to the ladder of the flying bridge. "It's not time to relieve me yet. There's an hour to go."

"I know," Track said, going up to join her. "I'm too restless to sleep. I guess it's the idea of taking on new supplies tomorrow."

Desiree laughed softly. "One would think you were the commander of a great naval squadron."

Track grinned. "Maybe my command isn't the biggest, but by God, it's the best—the very best."

"As part of the crew, I must agree," Desiree said.

Track sat down on the bench seat, and Desiree joined him. He looked closely at her in the soft yellow light. The shadows highlighted the woman's beautiful features and glinted delicately in her long, dark tresses.

"I love you, Desiree."

"I love you, Dan."

Track slipped his arm around her, and Desiree allowed herself to be pulled close to him. He kissed her tenderly, then gradually more intently until his tongue slipped between her soft lips.

Desiree returned his passion, moaning softly as she felt his hand slide into her blouse. "Oh, Dan!" she whispered, "what is becoming of us?"

As Track's desires grew, he fumbled at the buttons of her shorts. The woman helped him, quickly removing all her clothing. "Take me, Dan. It's what we both want. It will help us forget the quarrels and disagreements for a while."

Dan was soon as naked as she, and the two embraced, lying back on the bench seat entwined as Track slid into her, thrusting in a gentle persistent way that brought uncontrolled moans and sobs.

They peaked together, Desiree's arms locked tightly around his neck as she shuddered in release.

They stayed together for another few moments, then reluctantly parted. Still naked, they sat up. Track slipped his arm around her.

She smiled and softly caressed his face. *"Je t'aime,"* she said in French. "I love you with all my heart."

"I'm happy when we're together," Track said. "Perhaps we should admit that we belong together."

"Yes," she said. "We do." Then, in her own thoughts, she sadly added, *but, my darling, that's not what is destined to be.*

11

A hungry sea gull, searching for its breakfast, glided over Stubby Boudreaux's marina. Now and then the bird emitted an impatient cry as it scouted for food. The copperish light of a new dawning day shone weakly over the few boats moored at the weather-beaten docks as the feathered scavenger swooped and circled.

Stubby, a yawn on his whiskey-puffed face, fought to reach full wakefulness as he stepped from the door of his chandlery. His dirty khaki shirt was wide open, and the top button of his trousers was undone to allow his belly to expand. He scratched his hairy abdomen, then he belched and walked to the railing of the dock to spit into the fetid, oil-slicked water.

"Boudreaux!"

Stubby turned at the sound of his name. He saw two men he was slightly acquainted with. They were hangers-on at Pedro's Cielo Cubano bar up in Hobart. He was puzzled at their presence. "Howdy, fellers," he said uneasily.

Both individuals were big. Although not quite as large as Marvin Leroy Firpo, they were still damned impressive. The cheap silk-screened T-shirts they wore were completely filled out by muscular torsos. Stubby dully noted that one of the garments was inscribed Make Love Not War.

He smiled at the visitors as they approached him. But there was something about their manner that made him nervous. "What can I do fer you fellers? Y'all want a boat? Mebbe do some fishin'?"

"Nope," one said, "we brung you a message." They stood so close to Stubby by then that they were almost touching him.

"Y'all did, huh?" Stubby eyed him suspiciously. "Yore name is Darby, ain't it?"

"That's me," Darby said, grinning. He was a tough-looking blond man with thinning hair. "You remember ol' Dinkum here, don't you?"

Stubby grinned. "Sure. Howdy."

"Howdy," Dinkum said.

Stubby wiped his nose with the back of his hand in an uneasy gesture. He managed to grin again. "Well, now! So y'all got a message fer me, huh? Must be from that ol' Pedro."

"It ain't 'xactly from him direct," Darby explained, "but it came through him."

"Well, what's the word?" Stubby asked.

Darby's big fist shot out like a freight train steaming out of a railyard, slamming straight into Stubby's plump face.

Stubby staggered back and fell on his fat ass to the dock. He put his fingers to his nose and brought them back bloody. "What in the blue-eyed world did you do that for?"

"It's the message," Darby said.

Dinkum grinned. "And there's more."

Stubby, extremely fast for such a fat man, scrambled to his feet. "Y'all lemme 'lone, heah? I'm a vet'ran. The goddamn U.S. of American gummint's gonna git yore asses if y'all don't lemme 'lone!"

Darby responded with a quick charge that ended with a half dozen extremely hard open-handed slaps that again floored the marina operator. "We're supposed to let you know there's folks who're right pissed off with you."

Stubby, looking around wildly for his nephew, rubbed his stinging face. "Who's pissed off at me, goddamn it! An' why?" He was genuinely curious. "I ain't done nothin' wrong to nobody!"

"You sent a bad boat," Dinkum said.

"The hell I did!" Stubby protested. "I sent 'em two damn good boats—had rich folks on 'em, too! Good vessels, by damn!"

This time it was Dimkum who slapped him around. "That last boat was a bad'un."

Stubby thought quickly, then suddenly remembered. "The *Fancy Free*?" he asked. "Bullshit! It was a fine fuckin' boat, man!"

"I cain't argue with you none," Darby said, kicking at Stubby's scrotum. He missed, and the toe of his heavy shoe bit into the soft upper part of the marina operator's leg. "Seein' as how I ain't never laid eyes on her."

Dinkum slammed him hard with a left hook. "Me either. But I'd feel right in sayin' things din't work out none too good where that boat was concerned."

"Yeah," Darby said, throwing a hard bolo punch into Stubby's gut. "The damn boat musta been a dud."

Stubby was spun by a roundhouse from Dinkum that knocked him against the chandlery. He hit the coarse wood siding face first. "Oh, man, shit. Tha's enough, okay?"

"Nope," Darby said. He grabbed Stubby by the collar and banged him against the building three times. Then he flung him over to Dinkum.

Dinkum took hold of their victim's ears and brought his head crashing down to an uplifted knee.

"Oof!" Stubby was knocked upright, then he collapsed on the dock. "Hell, boys," he protested, "there ain't no damn boat *that* bad!"

"It musta been perty bad," Dinkum said. "We're gittin' paid a good hunk a dough to do a helluva job on you, Stubby."

"Yeah? How much'll you take to stop?"

"No, thanks," Darby said politely. He grabbed Stubby by the shirtfront and laboriously pulled him to his feet. "These fellers'd come after us if we din't do this right."

"Aw, hell, I wouldn't tell 'em nothin'," Stubby promised.

"Cain't do it, Stubby. Sorry." Darby's fist bounced three times off Stubby's face.

Stubby reeled back, his nose and mouth bleeding badly. He could barely see out of his rapidly swelling left eye.

"So yo're a vet'ran, huh?" Dinkum inquired with a punch to the side of the neck. "What outfit was you in?"

"Ar—my," he answered. Then Stubby, who had spent two years counting blankets at Camp Chaffee, Arkansas, added, "Korean...War." He hoped to elicit some sympathy—no matter how small the amount—from the gruesome twosome.

"Me an' Dinkum was in the Army," Darby said. He cut loose with a right jab and followed it up with a left hook.

By then, talking was more than Stubby could handle.

Dinkum stepped in and threw several lightning-fast punches that snapped Stubby's head back and forth. "We was in the artillery in Germany."

"It wasn't much, but a lot safer'n Vietnam," Darby said, starting to take his turn.

Then a booming voice from the rear caused him to pause.

"Y'all leave my Uncle Stubby be!"

Stubby saw Marvin Leroy. "Where...where," he wheezed, "in hell...have you...been...you, shithead, you!"

Marvin Leroy grinned and held up a string of catfish. "I been up to Snow's Creek. Looky what I got!"

"Fuck what you got!" Stubby said with his recovered voice. "Cain't you see what's goin' on here?"

Both Darby and Dinkum knew Marvin Leroy. They eyed him warily. "Howdy," Darby said.

The big kid was frowning again. "I want to know how come y'all are a-whuppin' on my Uncle Stubby."

Dinkum smiled. "We ain't!"

Stubby yelled so loud that bloody spit flew out of his mouth. "Hell, yes, they're a-whuppin' on my ass, you goddamned shithead! Now you get 'em both, boy!"

The two muscle men had seen Marvin Leroy in Pedro's bar a few times when the kid brought notes in from Stubby Boudreaux. They didn't know what kind of a fighter he was, but they weren't too anxious to find out. They stepped back a few paces.

"You just take it easy, boy. There's two of us," Darby cautioned him.

"Yeah," Dinkum added. "An' we ain't mad at you none, Marvin Leroy."

Stubby was furious. "Don't you lissen to them two sumbitches, Marvin Leroy! I tole you jump they asses—so you do it, boy!"

"Yes, sir, Uncle Stubby."

The boy moved forward rapidly, leaving the two men with two choices—fight or run.

Being Southern born and bred, they decided to fight.

Darby threw a straight right that hit Marvin Leroy's chest. The boy didn't even grunt as he reached over and grabbed his attacker's fist. He held him in a painful grip while kicking out at Dinkum as he rushed in.

Dinkum screamed when the size fourteen high-topped work boot slammed into his balls. He grabbed the pulverized family jewels and dropped to the dock howling.

Marvin Leroy swung a heavy open hand that collided with the side of Darby's head. The blow sounded like a shotgun—except to Darby, the ex-artilleryman, who would later swear someone had fired a 155 mm howitzer next to his ear.

Blood spurted from Darby's damaged ear and he went instantly and permanently deaf in it. His eyes rolled upward and he took three more of the hard cuffs until the lights went out.

Marvin Leroy dropped him to the dock. He looked at his uncle. "Now what?"

"Kick 'em bloody, goddamn it!" Stubby yelled in glee. The happiness he now felt overcame the pain he was in. "Go to it, boy!"

Marvin Leroy nodded his obedience and slammed a large foot into Darby. The big man flipped over and moaned before the twilight of unconsciousness enveloped him.

Stubby pointed to Dinkum. "Now him! Kick him, too, Marvin Leroy!"

Dinkum, wide awake, held up a hand in a silent gesture of mercy. He spoke in a strange, high-pitched voice. "Oh...no... don't do...nothin'....to me...please!"

But when Uncle Stubby commanded, nephew Marvin Leroy always obeyed.

The heavy shoe to the gut put Dinkum through the railing and into the dirty water of the harbor.

Stubby limped over to the edge of the dock and cackled down at the man who gamely treaded water despite his injuries. "That'll learn you, you sumbitch! They ain't nobody gonna come into *my* damn marina and kick *my* damn ass. If I ever see you or that fuckin' Darby again I'll shoot you both dead! *Dead! DEAD!*" He looked at Marvin Leroy. "Pull him outta there!"

"Yes, sir, Uncle Stubby." Marvin Leroy knelt down and reached out to grab Dinkum. He hauled him bodily from the water and deposited him on the dock.

Stubby slapped the injured man a few times. "Now you git aholt o'that damn Darby and drag his ass outta here."

Dinkum kept a wary eye on Marvin Leroy as he struggled to his feet, his groin a mass of pain. Slowly, with unsuppressed groans, he bent and grabbed Darby's collar to drag him away.

After the two enforcers were gone, Stubby led Marvin Leroy into the chandlery. He reached into the candy case and pulled out a Three Musketeers bar and tossed it to his nephew. "That's fer doin' good."

"Boy-oh-boy!" Marvin Leroy exclaimed, ripping the wrapper off. "My very most favorite!"

GEORGE BEEGH'S VOICE SOUNDED from below deck. "Blip on the radar screen—approaching fast. Has to be an aircraft."

Sir Abner, standing his turn at watch on the flying bridge, brought the powerful binoculars to his eyes. "That should be our delivery from The Consortium."

Track, sitting back on the companion bench seat with Desiree, checked his Rolex. "Right on time, too."

Sir Abner continued his vigil as George sung out the fast-decreasing range of the approaching object. Zulu appeared on deck with his Uzi held in his large hands. He smiled at his friends. "Just in case."

"Your ability to be ready for anything, anytime, is most admirable," Track said, grinning back.

George's voice sounded once again. "He should be in sight at any time now.

Suddenly Sir Abner exclaimed, "There he is!" He focused the binoculars as sharply as he could. "Good Lord!" he exclaimed.

Track and Desiree got up and rushed forward to join him. Zulu checked the Uzi.

"I feel like I'm in a bloody time machine." Sir Abner handed the binoculars to Track. "I do believe that's a PBY Catalina coming this way."

Track took but a couple of seconds to verify the Briton's sighting. "That's what it is, all right."

"I beg your pardon," Zulu remarked, "but evidently there is something here that is going over my head."

"It's an old World War II flying boat," Track explained. "They've been used for years, but you just don't see many of them anymore."

"They were real workhorses in their day, though," Sir Abner said. "Those Catalinas did everything from air-sea rescue to antisubmarine warfare."

"Let me see," Desiree said. She took the glasses and sighted them in on the approaching airplane. "It looks very big—oh! What are those ungainly glass bulges on the side?"

"Viewing ports," Sir Abner answered. "Observers would sit at them during missions." He laughed. "They also open wide to make beautiful entrances and exits. There were a couple of times in the war when I dove through them from a rubber raft with Jerry bullets singing about."

George came up the ladder. "He's made the proper countersign to the password. I've cleared him to come in."

Minutes later, the large aircraft skimmed in low on the water, finally touching down to make salty spray at its bow. Then it turned awkwardly in the water and floated toward them, moving in spurts of speed with each extra rev of its engines.

In the meantime, Sir Abner had started the diesels on the *Fancy Free* and helped close the distance. By skillful maneuvering, he moved slowly alongside as Track, Zulu and

George went about the tricky business of tying up to the plane in the briny wind behind its props.

Finally all engines—airplane's and boat's—were cut and the Caribbean was silent again. A man appeared at the nearest side window and opened it, pushing it outward. He grinned and waved at them. "How y'all doing?" He was a slender man with straw-colored hair and blue eyes. He wore a faded orange U.S. Navy aviator's flight suit and cowboy boots. A soiled white Stetson was pushed back on his head.

Track looked at him. "What part of Texas are you from?"

"Texas, hell! I'm from Oklahoma," the pilot said. "Kiowa O'Keefe's the name."

Track leaned down and stuck his hand in to grasp O'Keefe's. "Dan Track. I presume you have some things for us."

"Sure do." He pointed at a crate on the aircraft deck. "And I'll need some help with that baby. She weighs about eighty-plus pounds."

"Sounds like a Browning .50 heavy machine gun," Track said brightly.

"Sorry about that, partner," O'Keefe said. "This here's one of them limey jobs—a Vickers .303 caliber, as a matter of fact."

Sir Abner's voice sounded from the boat. "Good show! A Vickers, hey?"

Track hid his disappointment. "As long as we can mount it in the afterdeck salon."

O'Keefe nodded. "No sweat, pardner. Let's get to work. I got all kinds of goodies for you folks. Everything from vittles and water to bullets."

Track liked the way O'Keefe jumped into action. The pilot began passing crates and boxes out of the fuselage of his aircraft as the *Fancy Free*'s crew formed a human chain to transport the material aboard and set it on the deck.

A half hour later, Track and O'Keefe pushed and wrestled the crated machine gun from the Catalina to the motor yacht.

O'Keefe wiped at the sweat that dripped down his face. "That's it, pardner," he said. Again he offered his hand. "So long. I'll see you folks the next time you need a load." He waved up at the others. "Stay in touch," he hollered.

Track leaped back aboard the *Fancy Free* while Zulu and George let loose the lines that bound ship and plane together. He waved goodbye and ducked the salty spray as O'Keefe gunned the engines and drew away for takeoff.

The crew of the *Fancy Free* watched the PBY Catalina leave the water and slowly fight its way skyward. Sir Abner nodded his head in approval. "Quite a chap there, what?"

Track laughed out loud as he remembered the pilot's introduction. "Yeah. While we were in there working, he told me he was half Irish, half Scottish and all Oklahoma."

"I should think he would be quite handy if some rather sticky flying was required," Sir Abner commented.

"Could be," Track allowed. He looked at the equipment on the deck. "Well, let's get this stuff stowed. In the meantime I'll see to the machine gun. Once that baby is installed, locked and loaded, we're going pirate hunting."

12

The small armada of three motorboats cruised out of the anchorage of Ile-a-Salut an hour before daylight. Bonfires flickered on the beach as the sailors' women waved worried farewells to their men.

The losses of the boats over the previous two weeks had caused much consternation in the criminal community. The fact that one had been found badly damaged with its dead crew aboard had caused such an uproar that the mood of violence and lust for revenge in the community was barely containable.

Confidence in Philippe Matamore's leadership was more than a little shaken.

To make matters even more complicated, a dozen women had lost their men, that is, their meal tickets, and the presence of these free agents badly affected the morale of the others.

Eight of these ladies found immediate replacements on the island; one planned to return to a former boyfriend in Cartagena; another planned to visit her parents in Colon, Panama—she was extremely bitter about her lover's fate. But two of the ladies, who had no place to go, were unable to situate themselves with other men right away. They were forced to sell themselves to passers-through who sought sexual gratification during short, temporary stays on the island.

The people on the beach waited until the sounds of the departing boats were drowned by the distant surf on the other side of the harbor before they returned to their homes.

The commander in chief of the outward-bound force, the Tonton Macoutes agent Philippe Matamore, sat on the flying bridge of the Hatteras 72 Motor Yacht he had chosen as his flagship. Lagging slightly behind was a thirty-eight-foot Bertram Special Sport Fisherman, and the scout of the squadron, a feisty and speedy Magnum 63 Flybridge, swept out to the front. This craft would surge ahead, keeping in radio contact, to quickly investigate any radar blips that might pop up on the Hatteras's screen.

These vessels, as sleek and proud as any that could be found in the most exclusive marinas, were not standard in any sense of the word. Originally stolen from their murdered owners, they had been painstakingly converted to raider-smuggler craft.

These three craft had been intended to be the *corps d'elite* of the narcotics enterprise. Rather than being used only to run the gauntlet of the U.S. Coast Guard and Customs Service, they were destined to stay in international waters, using their sophisticated equipment and specially trained crews to direct, protect and monitor the activities of lesser vessels. As floating command posts, they would add safety and effectiveness to smuggling operations.

But the mysterious *Fancy Free* had forced Matamore to alter those plans. He now had to risk these expensive boats in an all-out effort to seek and destroy the vessel that had done in three of his crews.

Matamore was no sailor. Strictly a city slicker, he had left the seagoing activities to those more atuned to it. A bullyboy, gunman and secret policeman, he had other talents he could employ to maintain command of his criminal gang. But with boats and men missing in attacks obviously directed his way, Matamore's control over his cutthroats had begun to falter.

There had already been a couple of veiled threats. Insolent stares and whispers behind his back warned Matamore of the possible danger he faced. An organization like his was not run on democratic principles. A change of leadership was not a matter of election; it was brought about through elimination.

An open challenge, if not properly slapped down, could lead to Matamore's murder. So could losing the confidence and fear of his underlings. He had to demonstrate that it was a fatal mistake to oppose him.

That was the main reason for that predawn sailing.

The captain of the Hatteras Motor Yacht, a portly sea veteran named Leroux, made a final check on the radio-navigation gear, then walked over to the side to join Matamore. He pointed to the pink glow off the stern. "The sun is coming up, *chef*."

Matamore ignored the attempt at friendly conversation. "You have made arrangements to keep the radar going at all times?"

Captain Leroux nodded. "Yes, *chef*. There are three fellows down there pulling watches of two hours on and four off. Nothing will escape them."

Matamore tried to light a cigarette, but the stiff breeze kept blowing out his fancy lighter.

"You need one of these, *chef*," the skipper said. He pulled a Zippo Windproof from his pocket and flipped it open. A blue-and-yellow flame leaped to life.

Matamore leaned forward and lit his cigarette. "You are sure of this crew?"

"Of course," Leroux said. "I have sailed with them many times. And this yacht is a fine vessel, too."

"I'm sure it is," Matamore said caustically. "We took it from a wealthy New Yorker, *n'est-ce pas*?"

"But he was no *matelot*—seaman," Captain Leroux said. "A real amateur, that one."

"What about the radar crew?"

"An excellent bunch," the skipper said confidently. "The chief operator is American trained. He even went to the United States Naval school in Virginia when he was in the Mexican Guardia de la Costa. He's had experience on all the latest equipment."

"I want that *Fancy Free*," Matamore said with a menacing tone in his voice. "I will deal severely with anyone who makes mistakes and bungles this search."

"Don't worry, *chef*. We have a personal stake in this, too. As a matter of fact, Jorge, Humberto and Henri were close friends of mine," Leroux assured him. "If the *Fancy Free* is on the Spanish Main we will find her."

GEORGE BEEGH STRUGGLED with the open-end wrench, pulling until it was impossible to make the heavy bolt move another millimeter. He looked up from his task of anchoring the machine gun stand to the deck of the after-deck salon.

The sweat dripped freely from George's face and drained down his naked chest. "Whew! She's ready now, Dan."

Track, sitting on the settee with Desiree, stood up and walked to the other side of the room and leaned over to grasp the forty-five pounds of Vickers machine gun. He wrestled it up into his muscular arms and struggled over to the stand and set it into the grooves. As he did so, Sir Abner deftly inserted the locking lever and pushed it down, making a solid connection.

Track, like George, was perspiring heavily. "I didn't know this damned gun was water cooled. Adding that liquid puts another six or seven pounds onto the thing."

"It is, nevertheless, an excellent weapon," Sir Abner said. "I've sent many an ammunition belt through this gun—and every bloody shot was fired with complete confidence, believe me!"

"I believe you," Zulu assured him. "It is a formidable firearm, no doubt." He gave it a quick gunrunner's appraisal. "It is an easy-to-sell item. In fact, several South American armies have many in their arsenals."

"Then why don't they make 'em anymore?" Track asked.

"Too expensive," Zulu answered.

"Anyway, I don't like this water jacket bit," Track complained. "In fact—"

"Now, Dan, old son," Sir Abner interrupted. "May I remind you that the cooling feature makes the gun capable of heavy continuous firing?"

Track relented a bit. "Well, perhaps it isn't a bad choice."

Zulu grinned. "There is another item as well, Major. I have inspected the ammunition. It is Mk 8z .303 rounds, which are nitrocellulose loaded."

George was curious. "So?"

"That will add another thousand yards to the normal range of two thousand," Zulu explained.

"That's a pretty good reach," George said as he turned toward his uncle.

"Well, that's all fine and dandy," Track said with a scowl, "but this goddamned thing better shoot."

Sir Abner stepped forward. "Allow me."

The dapper Englishman went to work adding shims behind the adjustment nut on the lock-connecting rod to set up proper headspace. "Most important," he said as he worked. "Too much and one ruptures cases, not enough and the blessed thing will keep the lock from moving forward all the way."

Track nodded. "I understand headspace."

"Really?" Sir Abner asked in pseudosurprise. "Jolly good! That should make you all the better as gunner." After finishing, he got a box of ammo and locked and loaded one of the brass-studded canvas belts that held 250 rounds. "Here we go," he announced.

They all clapped their hands over their ears as Sir Abner fired a couple of short bursts.

"That bloody fusee spring wants some doing," Sir Abner said. He adjusted it between three more firings, then stepped back. "She is now ready for your stern appraisal," he said with a gesture toward Dan.

Dan walked up to the machine gun and grasped the firing handles. He pressed the trigger, and the heavy machine gun recoiled hard in rhythmic slamming against the restraint of the stand. By keeping his firebursts to six rounds, Track found he had excellent control. He worked the weapon through its entire firing arc of sixty degrees.

"Okay," he said. "We'll make do with it." After clearing the weapon, he turned his attention to the ammunition. "This is all armor piercing like I requested, but the tracer rounds were sent in a separate crate. Let's get into those belts and pull out every sixth round and replace it with a tracer."

"Jolly good idea," Sir Abner said. "That should help you to see where your fusillades are going."

"Right," Track said. "I might start some fires, too."

Desiree yawned and stretched from her position on the couch. "Going to roast chestnuts, *chéri*?"

Track grinned. "How about pirate nuts?"

MATAMORE LEFT THE FLYING BRIDGE and went below as soon as the sun grew hotter. He hated the pitching and rolling of the yacht. The constant wind out in the open did not help his disposition, either. He'd even been forced to abandon his white tropical suit and settle for more humble attire—tank top, shorts and sandals. The only luxury he could have aboard the vessel was his beer—but not in frosted mugs. They'd had to store too much food and there hadn't been room for that indulgence in the vessel's two refrigerators.

The physical discomfort and his brooding about the *Fancy Free* put Philippe Matamore in a bad mood.

He looked out at the monotonous, watery horizon and the spray that splashed by the porthole. With nothing to do, he now wished he'd brought Madeleine along. It would be nice to be in one of the berths with her, locked together with those firm thighs wrapped around his waist, while he took his pleasure.

"Chef!" Captain Leroux's voice broke into Matamore's sexual fantasy.

"What is it?" he asked irritably.

"There is a radar blip that looks promising," Leroux said. "It appears to be moving at the speed of a fast motorboat."

"Keep me posted," Matamore said. He finished his beer and tossed the bottle out the open porthole. Then he settled back to take Madeleine again in a mental orgy of sex.

Fifteen minutes later, Leroux again interrupted him. "We have spotted the boat, *chef*. From this distance it seems to match the description we have of the *Fancy Free.*"

"C'est bon," Matamore said in a better mood. He got up and went over to the small desk by the forward bulkhead. After strapping on a belt and holster holding his favorite .45 auto, he went up the ladder and joined Leroux on the flying bridge.

"Want to see?" Leroux asked, handing him the binoculars.

Matamore shook his head. "I will wait until we are close enough."

Leroux nodded, then placed the glasses to his own eyes. "She is a beauty—and fast, too."

Matamore was growing impatient. "You have not contacted her?"

"My radio operator says her receiver must be turned off," Leroux said. "They will see us soon, however, and react."

Matamore eagerly wet his lips. "Are the men ready?"

"Of course, *chef*," Leroux said. "My mate has seen to that." He continued to look at the strange boat. "What is the nationality of the boat we seek? American or Canadian?"

"American, of course," Matamore replied irritated. "Why do you ask?"

"I can see the ensign on their stern," Leroux said. "It bears the maple leaf insignia."

"Perhaps they are trying to fool us by flying Canadian colors," Matamore said. "Continue to approach them."

"Of course—ah! They are slowing and hailing us."

The vessels were now close enough that Matamore could make out four people in the cockpit. All were waving.

Within a quarter of an hour, Leroux had drawn the Hatteras motor yacht alongside the stranger. He turned the wheel over to his first mate and went to the side of the bridge while Matamore waited by the control console.

"Hello!" Leroux called out in a friendly voice. He could see an older man with a younger one and a woman. "We are the *Dolphin* out of Santo Domingo."

A middle-aged man, as round and full as Leroux, answered back, "Ahoy, *Dolphin*! We are the *Adventurer* out of Vancouver, Canada. We're doing a world cruise. We've just come out of the Panama Canal and, as a matter of fact, we're heading for your home port. Going there yourself?''

"Not at this time. We are looking for a friend," Leroux said. "An American vessel called the *Fancy Free*. Have you seen her?''

"Sorry. Can't say that we have."

Before Leroux could say anything further, Matamore walked up to the bridge rail. The Canadian started to give a greeting, but lapsed into a puzzled silence at the appearance of the armed man. Matamore, menacing behind the dark glasses, stared down at the three people for several long seconds.

The younger man slipped an arm around the woman. "Do you have any message, if we should see your friend?''

Leroux smiled and shook his head. "No. We are planning something of a surprise for them."

The Canadian laughed. "Then we shall most certainly say nothing to them." He looked at Matamore, his unease in the other's presence growing. "Is there anything we can do for you at all?''

Matamore wordlessly drew the pistol and aimed it at the speaker. He fired, hitting the man in the throat. He quickly swung to the older man and shot him in the head.

The woman was silent for one shocked moment, then she began to scream. Matamore, angered by the sound, sent three rapid shots into her body.

The sea, except for the chugging of boat engines, was strangely quiet as the echoes of the shooting died off.

Matamore reholstered the pistol. He looked at Leroux. *"Continuez la cherche."*

Then he went below for another beer.

13

In the bayou country of Louisiana, the people firmly believe that there are three *don'ts* to observe, if you wish to lead a long and happy life:

Don't take your pirogue out into a hurricane.

Don't stick your head in an alligator's mouth.

And most important, don't get a Cajun pissed off at you.

Pedro Rojas, owner of the Cielo Cubana Bar in Hobart, Florida, violated the third of those three rules when he followed orders from his higher-ups and sent Darby and Dinkum to beat up Stubby Boudreaux.

Stubby Boudreaux was a Cajun—and he was pissed off as hell at Pedro.

The anger that seethed in his short, fat body was evident in the way he now drove his Cadillac out of Key Largo across the causeway to the mainland.

Marvin Leroy Firpo sat on the passenger's side of his uncle's automobile, watching the scenery streak by the window as they sped north on Interstate One. "Hot dawg! You really got that ol' hammer down, Uncle Stubby."

Stubby, his fat cheeks swollen out even farther than usual by a combination of Red Chief chewing tobacco and a bruised jaw received in the beating he'd taken, spoke in a slightly muffled voice. "Damn right I got her down, boy. I'm on a sacred mission."

Marvin Leroy nodded his understanding. "Yo're gone whup on Pedro's ass, ain't you?"

"*Whup* on him? Did you say *whup* on him?" Stubby asked.

"Yes, sir, Uncle Stubby. I said that."

"You shithead, you! What the hell you think I got that Remington shotgun in the trunk for?"

Marvin Leroy shrugged. "We goin' huntin' after you whup Pedro's ass?"

Stubby sighed in exasperation. "When they passed out brains, you thought they said 'trains.' So you din' catch yours, did you, boy?"

Marvin Leroy wasn't real sure of what his uncle meant, so he went back to his original question. "Are you gonna whup on Pedro's ass, Uncle Stubby?"

"Hell, no! I'm gonna shoot that Cuban sumbitch!" Stubby shouted.

"Like you did my daddy?"

"Worse!"

"How could be it worser than that?" Marvin Leroy asked. "Daddy got kilt."

"Yore damn daddy was in one piece, wasn't he?"

"Yes, sir."

Stubby shifted the chaw. "Well, that damn Pedro ain't gonna be." He slowed down and took the exit for State Highway 27, heading west. "Gimme that whiskey, boy."

Marvin Leroy reached under the seat and pulled out the pint bottle of Southern Comfort. "Does this help the sore inside o' yore mouth, Uncle Stubby?"

"Sure do, boy," Stubby said. "Between this tobaccy and that likker, I'm damn near healed up physical. When that fucking Pedro is dead'ern a damn skinned 'coon, then my spirit's gonna be healed up, too." He angrily shoved the whiskey bottle back to his nephew. "Open this goddamn thing up. How'm I supposed to drive and pull the stopper?''

"Yes, sir." Marvin Leroy opened the bottle and returned it to Stubby. A sudden thought leaped into his slow mind, and he winced. "Do I gotta watch you blow ol' Pedro in two?"

"You gonna be there, boy, to back me up," Stubby said. "I don't want some sumbitch sneakin' up on me, unnerstand? You can look the other way while I go about the work of dismantlin' Pedro's carcass with that shotgun, but you keep yore eyes open for any sneakin' around by them pals o' his."

"Yes, sir, Uncle Stubby."

"I recall that they was always a feller out in the back alley behind the bar," Stubby said. "Was he there the last time I sent you to see Pedro?"

"Yes, sir. I seen him when I went out to take a pee," Marvin Leroy said.

"You went outside to pee, boy?" Stubby asked. "How come you din't use the pisser in the bar?"

"That's what that feller in the alley asked me," Marvin Leroy said. "I tole him 'cause they was somebody in there and I couldn't wait."

Stubby laughed. "Haw! At least you ain't so dumb you'd piss in yore pants, shithead."

Marvin Leroy grinned. "No, sir. I knew enough to go outside."

"As soon as you learn to come in outta the rain, you'll be a reg'lar Einstein, shithead."

"Yes, sir, Uncle Stubby."

A sign informed them that Hobart was five miles ahead.

"You ready, boy?"

Marvin Leroy nodded.

Stubby chuckled. "Okay, Pedro, you rum-drinkin', rhumba-dancin' sumbitch, say yore prayers. Cajun wrath is about to descend on yore squirrelly ass!"

THE CREW OF THE *FANCY FREE* lounged around the flying bridge enjoying the growing coolness as the Caribbean sun began its rapid descent to the western horizon.

Scorching, windless weather had marked the day, and even this slight drop in temperature was a welcome relief. Only George Beegh was not topside. It was his turn at radar watch, and he was below deck, clad only in shorts, his sweat-drenched face bent over the yellow-green light of the tube as he did his best to ignore the sweltering interior of his below decks station.

A sudden blip on the edge of the viewing screen caught his attention. Within five seconds he'd completely forgotten the discomfort. "Radar sighting!" he called out loudly. With all portholes and compartments wide open to let the evening breeze in, he was easily heard by his shipmates.

"Where away?" came Sir Abner's voice.

"Damn!" George said, grinning, "I love that sailor talk."

Track didn't bother to hide his irritability. "Where's that fucking blip?"

"Northwest," George quickly answered.

Topside, Zulu swung his binoculars in that direction. He swept the horizon off the port bow. "How far away is it, George?"

"To the outer limits of this little baby," George said, "about one and a half miles."

"Jesus!" George said. "The son of a bitch is closing in fast."

By then, Track had joined Zulu with his own binoculars. Several minutes passed, then Track pointed outward. "There she is! Damn, but George was right. She is a speedy little bitch."

Zulu studied the approaching boat. "She is heading directly our way. I have no doubt that she either has her own radar gear or is in contact with someone who does."

"I can see her quite well now," Track said. He whistled low. "That's a beautiful boat."

Zulu nodded his agreement. "It's a Magnum Flybridge. I feel I can speak without fear of contradiction when I say it is state of the art."

Track laughed aloud. "As big as you are, you can say just about anything without fear of contradiction."

"Well, never fear, Major, I shan't rely on my muscles to back up my claim," Zulu said, smiling. "As you can see, the boatmaker's name is on the side by the gunwale."

The speedboat came on rapidly, throwing out flying sheets of water from her bow, a white, churning wake following like a bubbling, porous sea monster. She took a wide turn and passed completely around the *Fancy Free*.

Finally Track was able to make out the crew. "All armed."

Sir Abner, straining with his binoculars, finally focused in on the men in the Magnum. "I believe you Yank chaps would describe that lot as 'hardcases.'"

George, now up on the bridge, added ominously, "'Real bad motherfuckers' is something else we'd call them."

Several incoming small-caliber rounds sang across the *Fancy Free*'s foredeck. Track and Company instinctively ducked.

George gritted his teeth in anger. "I think this is a time for that PZF44 rocket launcher."

"I agree," Track said. "Go to it, Tiger. I'll back you up rearward with the Vickers."

"Good show, lads! We'll teach the blighter!" Sir Abner exclaimed.

Wordlessly, Desiree and Zulu headed below to their Uzis as Sir Abner followed after them to take the battle-station controls located in the main cabin.

Track pulled the canvas cover from the machine gun and gave the weapon two good cranks. He waited until the speedboat came around the stern, then he pressed the trigger. The Vickers chugged out its five hundred rounds per minute, each sixth one a tracer. Track, still not very used to the weapon, finally scored a couple of hits just before the Magnum had pulled beyond his field of fire.

But George had his rocket launcher waiting.

He gave the correct lead, then pressed the trigger. In three seconds there was a blast of orange flame and the Magnum's bow blew apart.

The speedster came to such a sudden stop in the water that one of her crew was pitched forward into the sea.

"Swing around so I can finish the job," Track yelled up to Sir Abner.

"Right, old son."

The *Fancy Free* took a quick turn to port, and Sir Abner fought to compensate for the slide through the water as Track hosed the Vickers at the Magnum.

Pieces of the vessel flew around as hundreds of bullets slashed into her and the water in the immediate vicinity. After five minutes, Track abandoned the machine gun. He grabbed the SPAS-12 and raced onto the stern. "Back up to her, Sir Abner."

"Right you are, Dan!" The Englishman reversed both engines and slowly closed with the sinking Magnum.

Track, joined by Zulu and Desiree, stood on the stern. They could see one man hanging onto the floating wreckage. Three bodies were visible in the mess. Track leveled the shotgun. "Keep your hands in clear view," he warned the survivor.

"I don' take no shit from you, *Yanqui*!" the man screamed in rage. "We radio your position. Now our *jefe* on his way—he kill you."

"I admire your courage," Track said, "but your manners are appalling."

"Fuck you, gringo!" The man raised a hand holding an automatic pistol. He aimed it dead on the big American.

The SPAS-12 kicked back in recoil as it roared out a spreading charge of buckshot.

The pirate's body was lifted from the water to knee level and flipped over on its back. He had time for one spasmodic kick before he sank out of sight in the waters turned scarlet by his blood and gore.

The Caribbean was once again at peace.

By then it was almost dark. Zulu looked off into the inky distance. "Even with radar, they will not attack us in the night."

"You're right," Track said. "But tomorrow's gonna be one hell of a day."

STUBBY PARKED HIS CAR in the darkness at the end of the alley. As the fat man got out and walked around to the trunk, he could hear the noise of the crowd of people on the street who were enjoying an evening of diversion in the area's bars and brothels. Marvin Leroy joined him as he pulled the Remington pump out of its case. He operated the slide and chambered a round. "You 'member what I tole you, shithead?"

"Yes, sir, Uncle Stubby. When you nod yore head at me, I'm gonna smack the feller standin' there at the back o' the bar."

"Now we gotta be careful," Stubby said, looking down the alley. "The light around the door ain't too bright, but he's gonna see us walkin' up. Since he knows us, he won't figger nothin's wrong lessen he sees this here shotgun. I'll keep her behind me."

"Shouldn't we tiptoe, Uncle Stubby?"

"Goddamn it, you stupid asshole!" Stubby snapped. "I want the sumbitch to see us, 'cause they ain't no way we can sneak up on him. We want him to think we're just a-goin' in the back way."

"Yes, sir, Uncle Stubby."

"Okay. Now what're you gonna do when I nod at you?"

"Smack him a good'un."

"Right. Let's go."

Stubby, holding the shotgun muzzle down, kept it in tight to his fat ass as he and Marvin Leroy slowly approached the security man in the back of Pedro's bar.

Stubby spoke aloud. "It sure is a nice night, ain't it?"

"Huh?" Marvin Leroy said.

Stubby angrily whispered, "Just act natural and carry on a conversation like they ain't nothin' special goin' on."

"Okay, Uncle Stubby." Marvin Leroy cleared his throat and said loudly, "How long you had that shotgun, Uncle Stubby?"

Stubby stopped in midstride. His voice was strained as he struggled not to bellow in rage. "You goddamned-shit-for-brains-dickhead-shithead sumbitch!"

"Huh?"

By then they were halfway down the alley, and the guard was looking at them. Stubby forced a smile on his face and waved. "Howdy! Izzat you, Pablo?"

Pablo Ortiz squinted, his hand reaching inside his shirt. Then he relaxed. "Oh, I see who you are. Even in this dim light it is easy. Marvin Leroy is so big, and you so short and round, Stubby. How are you *muchachos*, 'ey?"

They walked up to the man.

"Somethin' wrong wit' your leg, Stubby?"

"I got a sore ass," Stubby said.

The Cuban laughed. "I bet you do. I hear you got it kicked."

Stubby nodded at Marvin Leroy.

Marvin Leroy was idly staring out onto the street at the passersby.

Stubby nodded again.

Pablo frowned in puzzlement. "You got a sore neck or somethin', Stubby?"

Stubby glared at Marvin Leroy. "I'm a-noddin' at you, shithead."

"Oh? Oh! *Oh!*" Marvin Leroy said in dawning realization. Then his big fist shot out in a blur, contacting solidly with Pablo's jaw.

The Cuban, his eyes rolled upward, danced off to the side and collided with the doorframe before spinning around and dropping to the dirt.

Marvin Leroy smiled uncertainly. "Did I do good, Uncle Stubby?"

Stubby growled. "You shithead, you!" He motioned and went up to the door, carefully opening it. "Now keep yore damn eyes open."

The back of the bar opened into a narrow hallway where the restrooms were located. Beyond that, a dozen feet short of the saloon proper, Pedro Rojas maintained his office. Stubby, with Marvin Leroy behind him, eased toward the door. He noted another guard standing at the entrance to the hall. The man, keeping a close eye on the activities in the bar, had his back to them.

Stubby glanced back at his nephew. "Keep quiet, hear?"

"Yes, sir, Uncle Stubby."

Stubby reached the office door and opened it. He quickly stepped inside and brought the shotgun up level.

Pedro Rojas looked up from his work on the desk. *"Que?"* His eyes opened wide and he instinctively stood up.

"Sit down, Pedro," Stubby commanded.

Pedro obeyed instantly. He even raised his hands without being asked. "'allo, Stubby. Wha's the big idea, 'ey?"

"I'll do the question askin' here," Stubby said. "Marvin Leroy, keep a eye out that door."

"Yes, sir, Uncle Stubby," Marvin Leroy said. He was glad he had an excuse to turn his face away from the carnage that was sure to follow.

Stubby glowered at Pedro. "Now I wanna know how come you sent Dinkum and Darby down to whup on my ass."

"What the hell you mean bargin' in here wit' that shotgun?" Pedro demanded. "I got my boys all aroun' here!"

"A fat lotta good they'll do you with yore ass splattered against the wall," Stubby said defiantly.

"They'd shoot you, too!" Pedro snarled.

"What the fuck do you care?" Stubby asked. "You'll already be dog meat."

"So will you," Pedro pointed out.

"But I'll still be satisfied," Stubby said. "Cajun justice is all I'm after. If it kills me, I don't care. It's a matter o' honor."

Pedro knew he was serious. "Now, now, Stubby. I know you pissed off for me. But it wasn't my idea, Stubby," Pedro said fearfully. "I was told to have 'em do it."

"Then you ain't got nothin' to worry about, Pedro," Stubby said. Then he added ominously. "Providin' you let me know who tole you to do it."

Pedro shrugged as best he could with his hands up. "You know I can't do that, Stubby. I'd be wasted for giving out a name."

Stubby pushed the shotgun forward. "Yo're damn well gonna git wasted if'n you don't tell me—and do it now! And you better not lie, Pedro. The answer better make sense or I'll just give up on findin' out who it is—and blow yore damn ass apart.''

"Okay! Okay! I tell you, Stubby,'' Pedro said. The barrel of the pump Remington looked as big as a railroad tunnel to him. "It was Mr. Banks.''

Stubby thought for a moment then nodded. "Yeah—yeah, it'd have to be that sumbitch.''

Pedro felt a surge of relief. He even lowered his hands a little. "Yeah. It was Mr. Banks, Stubby. He made me do it, man.''

"Y'know, Pedro, I even thought it might be him before I came up here,'' Stubby said.

"Well, amigo, you was right. He's a powerful man. There wasn't nothin' I could do but obey him.''

"He's a big man, all right,'' Stubby mused. "So big, in fact, I'd never be able to touch him.''

"Tha's right,'' Pedro said.

"So since I cain't git him, I'll take it out on you,'' Stubby said.

Pedro laughed weakly. "You make the joke, eh, Stubby?''

Stubby laughed and pulled the trigger.

The Cuban took the full load in the throat and chest, the blast slamming him against the wall a millisecond after his insides splattered there. He toppled over, nearly blown in half.

Stubby pumped the slide and turned quickly to charge out the door. He fired in the direction of the barroom at the guard who had come running at the sound of the first shot.

The thug violently spun around three times before hitting the floor.

Stubby fled out the bar with Marvin Leroy behind him.

Outside, Pablo Ortiz sat dazed by the door. He had just started to get to his feet when Marvin Leroy charged outside and collided with him. The Cuban, knocked back to the pavement, once again sank into unconsciousness.

They ran down the alley to the car and leaped in. Stubby hit the ignition, then backed out into the street and sped back toward the main drag.

They continued on until they reached State Highway 27. Only then did Marvin Leroy speak. "Where we goin', Uncle Stubby?"

"Back home. Cajun honor is served, boy," Stubby said.

Marvin Leroy was silent for another few minutes. "Is ol' Pedro dead?"

"Yup," Stubby answered. "But I'm a little disappointed."

"What about, Uncle Stubby?"

"Technically speakin', I din't blow him in two," Stubby said sadly. "I noticed he was kinda held together by a coupla pieces o' skin." He thought about it for a few more minutes. "Y'know, that kinda ruins this whole fuckin' day!"

14

It had been a long sleepless night for the intrepid crew of the *Fancy Free*.

Even when off watch, they had taken only brief naps, short periods of dreamless sleep as they tossed and turned in their narrow bunks. At one time during the long hours of darkness—2:30 A.M.—all five members of Track and Company were awake and on deck. It was the pragmatic Sir Abner who got them to at least try to relax even if sleep was impossible.

"See here," he told them, "there's naught to be gained by all of us being stupid with sleepiness tomorrow. Even if one can't get some kip, one should lie abed and relax as much as is physically possible."

"I'm certain adrenaline will keep us awake during any fighting with pirates," George argued.

"You're absolutely right," Sir Abner allowed, "but what about that time before any excitement begins? The person on deck or radar watch might finally doze off from sheer fatigue. A matter of minutes could prove quite fatal, what?"

"I agree wholeheartedly, Sir Abner," Zulu said.

"So do I," Track added. "But it's easier said than done."

"I tell you what," Sir Abner suggested. "Let's play a game my nanny taught me."

"Nanny!" George Beegh crowed. "You had a nanny— a *nanny*!"

"Of course, my boy," Sir Abner said defensively, "part of an English gentleman's upbringing, don't you know?"

Desiree did not appreciate George's attitude. "Having a nanny," she said coldly, "obviously produces a sensitive and gentlemanly adult male."

"Maybe so," George said, laughing softly. "A nanny! Did she tuck you in bed every night?"

"As a matter of fact she did. And that has a bit to do with what I have to tell you," Sir Abner said. "My nanny taught me a little game that helped tremendously in getting me to sleep. She would help me to relax by beginning with my toes. She would say to me, 'Toes, relax.' Then I would concentrate getting my toes to relax. Then she'd go to the ankles, shins, knees, and so on until she reached my head. By then I would be asleep. It worked quite well actually, and I might add that I was a rather active and alert little boy."

George had hooted a bit more at being under the care of a little old lady. But when they went below to their bunks— with the exception of Track who was taking his turn at deck watch—they all listened intently as Sir Abner spoke in a soft voice:

"Toes, relax. Feet, relax, Ankles, relax—" He used a singsong tone. He was finally saying, "Chest, relax" when a loud snore broke out in their midst.

It was George. He had fallen fast asleep.

Now, with the early-morning light slowly intensifying, everyone was on deck except for Desiree, who manned the radar in her turn.

George was as fresh as the proverbial daisy. He'd gotten a solid four hours' snooze and felt great. "I'll tell you something," he said to Sir Abner. "There'll be no more laughing at nannies from me."

"I should hope not," Sir Abner responded.

Zulu laid a hand on the young man's shoulder. "You should always remember, George, that many times there're valuable lessons to be learned in situations that are not immediately comprehensible or appreciated."

George winked at the others. "I have to admit, though, if I was going to have a nanny, my choice would be a twenty-year-old with a nice ass."

Sir Abner laughed. "None of those dowdy types for you, hey, George?"

Before any further discussion of the subject could begin, Desiree shouted from her post below decks. "Radar blip to the south! Approaching fast!"

Track and Zulu, binoculars in hand, rushed to the rail of the flying bridge.

Desiree hollered again. "Now another from the north! Both are obviously closing in on us!"

"I think this is what we've been waiting for," Track said.

George wordlessly but with a great feeling of excited anticipation leaped over the ruined windshield to the foredeck. He wasted no time in opening the hatch of the forepeak and getting inside to prepare his rocket launcher.

Sir Abner led Track and Zulu below. The Englishman took his post at the control console while Zulu picked up his Uzi submachine gun and joined Desiree at their appointed places.

Track went directly to the Vickers and gave the heavy weapon a cursory check. He cranked the charging handle twice, then cut loose with a couple of test bursts.

"Crew report!" Track yelled.

"Helmsman ready!" Sir Abner answered.

"Starboard gunner ready!" Zulu yelled.

"Port gunner ready!" Desiree reported.

"Rocket launcher ready!" George hollered. "Bring 'em on!"

"An unnecessary request," Sir Abner said, looking at the radar screen on the control console. "They'll be here with us in a matter of minutes."

Within less than a quarter of an hour, the boats were close enough to be seen by physical observation.

George, peering out of the forepeak, emitted a low whistle. "Wow! Those are some heavy dudes!"

Track left the machine gun to join Sir Abner. He used his binoculars for a closer look at the boat approaching from the north. "Jesus! Those bastards are loaded for bear."

"What about the other blighters?" Sir Abner asked.

Track went back to the stern and focused the glasses on the vessel closing in from that direction. "And those sons of bitches are loaded for elephant. I think it can be safely assumed they're looking for trouble."

Sir Abner nodded grimly. "There's but one thing to do in a case like this."

"What's that?" Track asked.

"We must go to war, old son," Sir Abner answered.

Tracked nodded. "Then let's go."

Sir Abner punched up the motors, then opened both throttles as he engaged the clutches. The *Fancy Free* surged forward, then picked up speed.

From that point on, the battle would be led indirectly by Sir Abner's whims, based on the shouted directions from the others. He would listen for these suggestions, but it was his ultimate responsibility to maneuver the craft to the most advantageous positions during the fight. He would have to provide the maximum opportunities for Track to use the Vickers off the stern, yet keep in mind the value of George's rockets that would be fired from the bow.

Sir Abner could see that the nearest vessel—which also happened to be the largest—was a Hatteras Motor Yacht. He had no doubt it had been modified for combat.

When the quad-fifty Browning heavy on the flying bridge erupted into four-barrel volleys that splashed toward them in a rapid testing of range, he knew the *Fancy Free* was in for the fight of its life. He put the boat into a slow but steady turn to give Track an opportunity to return fire.

Track pressed the trigger repeatedly as he swung the gun through its arc. He tried to get through the superior firepower that was directed at them. When he could no longer see the target through the afterdeck salon windows, he shouted, "Give George a chance!"

"Right you are," Sir Abner said cheerfully. He took a hard turn to port.

George aimed rapidly and fired. The shot remarkably accurate for being launched so quickly and unexpectedly.

But it failed to score.

A watery explosion on the other side of the raider boat marked the miss.

Sir Abner, aware that the *Fancy Free* was a large target while traveling parallel with the other vessel, spun the wheel to starboard.

"Another bandit dead ahead!" George yelled.

"Want a shot?" Sir Abner inquired calmly.

"I thought you'd never ask," George said. He quickly reloaded and connected another rocket into the firing mechanism.

The second enemy boat was a Bertram Sport Fisherman. Slower than both its companion craft and the *Fancy Free*, it made up for its lack of speed with the 57 mm antitank cannon mounted on its armored flying bridge. The two-man crew serving the weapon knew their business.

A sudden whine and crash of glass alerted Sir Abner to the problem. A second whine was followed instantly by an explosion on the port side of the *Fancy Free*.

Sir Abner fought the wheel as the vessel rolled wildly from the impact. The Englishman, nearly deaf in his left ear, shouted as he regained control, "Assess the damage!"

Zulu went farther below into the lower cabin and checked the bulkheads. He climbed back up the ladder. "No leaks."

"Thank God for large favors!" Sir Abner said. He gripped the wheel. "Dan, get ready!"

"Ready!"

Sir Abner violently turned the wheel to starboard, letting it spin freely, as he pulled back on the port throttle and revved up the starboard engine.

The *Fancy Free* made as tight a U-turn as possible, sending out a spray of water. Track sent several firebursts cutting through the artificial geyser, using the tracers to check the accuracy of his aim.

A figure by the antitank cannon suddenly stood erect and grasped his chest. He staggered to one side and pitched over the railing into the sea. Track started to cheer, but noted that another man quickly took the lost crewman's place.

Track gritted his teeth, his mind speaking his feelings. *This ain't gonna be easy!*

Now they were heading back toward the Bertram. George stood in the forepeak hatch, the rocket launcher ready. "Veer off a bit!" he hollered.

"Right!" Sir Abner snapped, acknowledging the suggestion. He had evened the throttles and was on a steady course. He gave the wheel a slight turn to port. George aimed dead on the unfriendly vessel.

The pirates' quad-fifty pumped .50-caliber slugs at the approaching *Fancy Free*. George could hear the heavy rounds slapping the air around his head and zinging off the bow rail.

He held his aim steady and fired.

The rocket flew from the tube across the expanse of water to strike into the Hatteras Motor Yacht windscreen. But it passed on through, exploding fifty meters beyond the target.

The quad-fifties stepped up their fusillade, and George ducked.

Sir Abner didn't need any urging to take up an evasive pattern. The *Fancy Free* zigzagged and waggled out of range.

But now the Bertram had closed in on them again.

The antitank cannon pumped more rounds their way. The after bulkhead of the salon exploded. Track felt his breath swept away, and he was flung through the door and down into the lower deck. He landed flat on his back, the wind knocked out of him.

"Chéri!" Desiree cried. She rushed to him, helping her lover to sit up. "Are you hit?"

Track tried to speak, but could only gasp.

Zulu quickly examined Track. "I can find no wounds other than some abrasions."

Track wiped his nose, which was now bleeding. "Uh—oof! Concussion...damn...it..."

Zulu grasped the man under the arms and hauled him to his feet. "We received a hit on the stern, right?"

Track nodded. "Right...I...got...to...get...back." He struggled up the ladder with Zulu following. By the time he'd returned to the machine gun, his breathing was back to normal. He inspected the area where the bulkhead had been. A gaping hole, with part of the settee

blown away, was all that was left. "They've got light artillery of some sort."

"I heard the rounds," Zulu said. "I estimate it at less
than 70 mm ammo."

Track pointed to the extensive damage. "Christ! I'm
glad it's no bigger."

"Expert gunners can make up for light ordnance," Zulu
said.

Sir Abner's voice interrupted them. "Watch it on the
bow, lads. The bastard's outflanked me."

Track looked up to see the Hatteras Motor Yacht suddenly appear to their stern. The quad-fifty aboard her
flashed as the four-barreled weapon fired screaming .50-
caliber death in their direction.

The overhead in the salon exploded into splinters and
the air was filled with the roar and ricochet of incoming
rounds. Track fought an instinctive urge to slam himself
to the deck. Instead, he leaped to the Vickers and hosed
out a long stream of bullets straight into the bow of the
pursuing vessel.

The windshield of the Hatteras exploded, and she suddenly veered away. Zulu ran to the open window and
watched the pirate draw off. "Damn!" he exclaimed. "She
is still under control, Major."

Track grinned and patted the Vickers. "That's okay. We
showed her not to fuck with us."

The port side of the *Fancy Free* flamed up in a violent
explosion that rocked her so hard that both Track and
Zulu were pitched into the starboard settee.

"It's that bloody Bertram and those cannon again!" Sir
Abner shouted. He began evasive maneuvering.

Zulu, his face serious, looked into Track's eyes. "Things
seem to be getting a bit sticky."

Track nodded at the understatement and added one of his own. "It's going to be a long day."

Zulu smiled grimly. "If we're lucky!"

15

The door to Stubby Boudreaux's chandlery opened, and Marvin Leroy Firpo stuck his head inside. "Strangers is up at the head o' the dock, Uncle Stubby."

Stubby, a Smith & Wesson .45 revolver in a heavy holster strapped to the belt around his wide waist, loosened the weapon. He walked around the counter to the front of the store and took a cautious look from the window.

"Shit!"

He could see several husky well-dressed men standing beside a limousine parked by the curb. They were obviously casing the place, their gazes sweeping the entire area of the marina. After a few moments of observation, one leaned down to speak to somebody in the automobile's rear interior. After exchanging a few words, the dapper thug walked slowly down the dock toward the store.

Marvin Leroy frowned. Even his dull mind could comprehend what was going down. "Is them fellers out to hurt you 'cause you blowed up ol' Pedro?"

Stubby nodded. "There's a good chance o' that, boy." He nodded toward the far corner of the room. "Stand over there and stay in the shadows. If things get rough, you know what to do, don't you?"

"Yes, sir," Marvin Leroy said menacingly. "We gonna fight 'em, ain't we?"

"Just be cool, shithead!" Stubby cautioned him. "That guy's walkin' up here bold as he pleases. He ain't sneakin' around and neither are them others up there by that big ol' car. Maybe they don't mean no hurt." Then he added, "But on second thought, maybe they do." He took a dirty handkerchief from the back pocket of his soiled khaki pants and wiped at the beads of perspiration that were popping out on his fat face.

Marvin Leroy glanced out of the window. "I don't know who he is, Uncle Stubby. I ain't never seen him up to Hobart. Could be he ain't got nothin' to do with Pedro."

Stubby wet his lips nervously. "Yes, he does. I know his kind, boy. He's a knuckle-crunchin' sumbitch. You can bet he uses his muscle as a enforcer for the big shot that ol' Pedro was errand boy for."

The man stopped in front of the door. "Mr. Boudreaux?" His voice was clear and loud.

Stubby remained silent.

"Mr. Boudreaux, I got business with you." He unbuttoned his expensive coat and held it open to show he had no weapons. Not sure from which direction he was being observed, he slowly turned around in a complete circle.

Stubby hesitated, then pulled his pistol. "You wanna come in here?"

"Only if it's okay with you."

Marvin Leroy smiled. "He's right polite, ain't he?"

"Shut up, shithead!" Stubby growled at his nephew. Then he looked toward the door. "We're gonna let you in, but I want you to know I got a Smith & Wesson Committee of Forty-five to back me up. So you keep yore damned hands in plain sight, got it?"

"Yes, sir, Mr. Boudreaux."

Stubby nodded to Marvin Leroy. "Walk up real easy to the door and open her up—slow! You understand 'slow,' shithead?"

"Sure. That means don't do it fast." Marvin Leroy tiptoed up to the door and followed the instructions to the letter. Then he returned to his spot in the corner.

"C'mon in," Stubby invited the stranger. He raised the pistol and pointed it straight at the door.

The man, both hands spread wide, stepped inside. He hesitated when he saw the weapon, then he spoke in a friendly tone. "How're you doing?"

"Tolerable," Stubby answered. "Yoreself?"

"Fine. There's somebody here that wants to talk with you."

"Who might that be?" Stubby asked. He quickly added, "And who the hell are you?"

"My name's Garello. The man who wants to see you is my boss. Mr. Banks."

Stubby's eyes widened. "Mr. Banks—wants to see me?" He slowly lowered the pistol.

"Yeah," Garello answered, relaxing a bit. Then he caught sight of the hulking Marvin Leroy in the corner and tensed again. "We ain't here for trouble, Mr. Boudreaux. If we was, we couldn't come in broad daylight, and Mr. Banks wouldn't have showed up here hisself."

"Yeah," Stubby said, rubbing a nervous hand across his mouth. "I reckon he wouldn't." He took a deep breath and reholstered the revolver. "I'd be most pleased to see Mr. Banks. Should I go out to him?"

"He'll talk to you here," Garello said. "I'll get him."

"Sure, sure," Stubby said. "Go ahead."

Garello left and Marvin Leroy spoke in a puzzled tone. "Is ever'thing all right or what, Uncle Stubby?"

There was a slight quaver in Stubby's voice. "It don't matter, shithead. The fact we gotta face is that there ain't nothin' we can do about it one way or t'other."

Marvin Leroy decided to shut up and watch the proceedings.

The door opened again. Garello stepped in followed by a much smaller man. He was stoop-shouldered and skinny and appeared to be ill. His pale face was that of an old man, but the thinning hair showing under his Ivy League-type hat showed no traces of gray. He wore dark glasses, which seemed to highlight the gauntness of his appearance.

"How do, Mr. Banks."

Banks raised a hand in greeting. He wasted no time. "Did you kill Pedro Rojas?" His voice was low and raspy, like that of a man with weak lungs.

Stubby nervously tugged at the bill of his yachting cap. "Well . . . now, I did . . . sir—Mr. Banks."

Banks looked intently at the Cajun for a full minute before he spoke again. "He was one of my boys."

"Pedro had me whupped for no good reason." There was a hint of defiance in Stubby's voice. "I know you gave him the order, Mr. Banks. But it wasn't fair. I din't do nothing but my job, and you went too damn far on account of some kinda problems with a boat I tole Pedro about."

"That boat's been bad trouble," Banks said.

"That ain't my fault," Stubby protested. "I get paid fer pointin' out good vessels. That was the deal I made, and I stuck to it. If somethin' was wrong with the boat, it wasn't my fault."

Banks continued his expressionless gaze. "You figure I was unfair to you, huh?"

"Yes, sir, I sure as hell do."

"So you got angry and walked in and blew Pedro away?"

"I knowed what I was doin'," Stubby said. "I went in by the alley. He only kept one guard out there, and I knew the sumbitch. It wasn't hard to git in or out. I had my nephew there—'' he pointed to Marvin Leroy ''—smack him a good'un, then I went in.''

"Pedro was careless," Banks said.

"Yes, sir. After I shot him, I jumped back out into the hall and cut loose toward the bar where his other boy was," Stubby said. "Then I run outside and down the alley to my car."

"It was a nice hit," Banks said. "It was clean and fast. The newspapers said the cops didn't have any witnesses or suspects in the case."

"I din't do it to piss you off," Stubby said, "but I cain't let no man whup on me and not do somethin'." He edged a threat into his voice. "I cain't take that kind o' shit from nobody, Mr. Banks—nobody!"

Banks looked straight into Stubby's eyes. "Not even from me?"

Stubby hesitated. "I reckon there's a limit to ever'-thing, Mr. Banks. Yo're a powerful man. I know there ain't no place on God's green earth for me to hide if you decide to come after me."

"Everybody makes mistakes," Banks said. "Even me. Maybe I was wrong about your participation in this affair with the boat."

"Excuse me, sir, but you was," Stubby insisted.

"You have great physical courage and brains," Banks said in a flat tone.

"Thank you, sir."

"You took a bum rap, so I'll make it up to you," Banks said. "You got Pedro's job."

"Sir?"

"I'm turning his responsibilities over to you," Banks said.

"Thank you kindly," Stubby said as the full import of the offer sank in. "I don't want to be ungrateful, Mr.

Banks, but I got no real hankerin' to live up there in Hobart.''

"You don't have to," Banks said. "You can stay right here in your marina. It makes a good cover, particularly since you've been here for years. And you'll be paid well— quite well. Garello will come back later and fill you in on your duties and give you a half dozen gunsels to back up your ass.'' He laughed dryly. "I hope you make more efficient use of them than Pedro did.''

Stubby was too astounded to speak.

"So long, Mr. Boudreaux.''

"Call me Stubby.''

"Call me Mr. Banks.''

THE BOAT'S ENGINES IDLED, and the vessel rocked gently in the shallow swells of the Caribbean. Captain Leroux stood by the ladder leading below deck. *"Comment marchent les moteurs?''* he called.

"The engines are fine, *capitaine*,'' a crewman's voice from the interior assured him. "They were flooding, so I'm adjusting the carburetors.''

Leroux gestured to the damage inside the cabin. "We took quite a few hits, *chef*. I want all the damage inspected before we take up the fight again. It wouldn't be an ideal situation to be charging toward that devil boat and suddenly find us stopped dead in the water. It's bad enough when we're moving.''

"He'll get away," Matamore complained mildly.

But Leroux shook his head. *"Mais non, chef*. Platas is playing the cowboy on the Bertram, and keeping him running back and forth in the area. Besides, if he tries to give us the slip, it will show up on the radar screen.''

A dead man, the helmsman, lay in one corner of the cabin where Leroux had rolled him during the heat of the battle. Three ugly wounds where machine gun slugs had slammed into his body still drained blood onto the deck where shards of glass from the windshield were scattered.

Leroux looked at the corpse. "I don't know who the bastard is that's handling their machine gun, but he can sure shoot." He gave the damage another quick assessment. "I don't think that last long burst wavered more than half a yard when it smashed through here."

Matamore had stood motionless when the cabin exploded in the hail of slugs. A few pieces of flying glass had cut his face slightly, and his tank top was speckled with small flecks of his own blood.

Leroux laughed. "You're a cool one, *chef*. When those volleys crashed in here, I was on the deck so fast I don't even remember ducking. I looked up at you, and you were just standing there like a bit of breeze had blown in."

Matamore ignored the compliment. "Have someone bring me a beer." He lit a cigarette.

"Of course, *chef*." He went back to the ladder and shouted to the men working below. *"Apportez une bière au chef."*

A moment later a Hispanic sailor appeared with a cold bottle of brew. He handed the bottle to his chief and took note of the cuts and the blood on his shirt. He grinned. "I hear you spit in their faces, *jefe*."

Matamore knew that his personal performance in the fight would be the final determination of whether he retained control of his small empire. So far he'd impressed the men, but he knew he needed a clear victory to give him unchallengeable dominance again. Matamore took a sip of beer. "Before this is over, I'll do more than spit at them."

"Certainement, chef!" Leroux said with a laugh. He looked at the crewman. "How soon can we be under way?"

"Another half hour, *capitaine*," the sailor answered. He nodded a curt farewell and went back below to join in the work.

Leroux sighed. "We may be at this for quite a while longer, and it's growing hot." He walked over to the corpse and bent to pick it up. He staggered out of the cabin onto the afterdeck and unceremoniously dumped the dead man into the sea. "Marcel was a good man, but he would soon start stinking in the heat," he explained, returning inside.

A voice from above suddenly sounded. "The quad-fifty is checked out, *capitaine*. A fresh load of ammo is stowed and we are ready to go."

"Right," Leroux said. He pointed at the overhead. "That is one of the best weapons in the world."

"Of course," Matamore said. "I shall be most happy when we are in a position to use it again."

"Don't worry, *chef*," Leroux assured him. "We will be soon."

The Hispanic sailor reappeared. "We are ready to start up."

"Fine," Leroux said. He went to the control console and punched the starter, easing the throttles forward. The motor kicked over and hummed out as the rpm increased.

"It sounds good to me," Matamore said with the hint of a threat in his voice.

The menacing tone wasn't wasted on Captain Leroux. "Everything is fine, *chef*. Here we go." He engaged the clutches, and the vessel moved forward in the water, picking up speed as more acceleration was applied.

The quad-fifty above them fired a couple of test bursts.

Matamore displayed a rare smile. "Now let's move in and finish off those bastards on the *Fancy Free*."

16

Zulu, wearing a wide-brimmed straw hat to protect himself from the unrelenting pounding of the searing sun, stood on the companion bench seat of the *Fancy Free*. He pressed a pair of heavy binoculars against his eyes as he painstakingly surveyed the horizon on all the compass points.

Desiree Goth, below deck on radar watch, wiped at the sweat that trickled down her face and throat to flow in small rivulets between her breasts. Her long hair was pulled back in a ponytail in an effort to beat the heat.

The glow of the cathode tube was a dull green and was blank, as it had been since dawn when she'd taken over the chore from George Beegh. Desiree could hear the footsteps of the rest of Track and Company as they went about the business of preparing their vessel for the expected upcoming action.

Suddenly dual blips appeared on the far edge of the screen. Desiree wasted no time in shouting the alarm. "Two sightings to the stern! Approaching fast!"

Dan Track, who had been tending to cleaning the Vickers in the afterdeck salon, quickly slid down the ladder and joined her. A few seconds later Sir Abner arrived.

Track watched the blips for a minute. "They're spreading out a bit."

"Right," Sir Abner agreed. "Looks like they want to attack us on both flanks."

"And simultaneously," Desiree added.

"Either that or herd us along toward some destination," Track said. "At any rate, it makes no difference what their plans are. Whether they hit us straight on or try some fancy strategy, we'll simply play the game by ear."

"In other words," Sir Abner surmised, "we shall respond in an appropriate manner to whatever they try against us, right?"

"Right," Track said.

Sir Abner calmly noted the speed of the approaching bandits. "I suggest we all get to our places immediately."

"If not sooner," Track added.

The *Fancy Free*'s crew, now well drilled, quickly reported to their battle stations. Sir Abner went into the main cabin. He kept his eyes on the auxiliary radar at the control console, as he eased the throttles forward a bit and engaged the clutches. The boat started slowly through the waves, then gained speed.

Track cranked the Vickers and swung it through its firing arc. George Beegh, in the forepeak, rechecked the stowage of his rockets to make sure they would be within easy reach. Then he, like the others, settled down to wait.

Desiree, forgetting the oppressive wet heat, continued to monitor the main radar. "Closing in fast," she announced. "They should be in sight within five or six minutes."

Sir Abner checked the chronometer above the control console and waited for exactly three minutes to pass. Then he shoved the throttles all the way forward to bring the *Fancy Free* to full speed. He didn't want to give the two pirate vessels any advantage when the engagement began.

"They are falling back a bit," Desiree announced.

Sir Abner slowed down enough to allow them to catch up. The *Fancy Free* was on no escape-and-evasion operation. Her mission was contact and destroy.

"There they are!" Zulu announced upon sighting them. Then he rushed below deck.

Desiree leaped up from the radar set and grabbed the Uzi that was sitting beside her. She hurried to her battle position on the port side opposite Zulu.

Zulu grinned at her, his white teeth flashing in his ebony face. "It appears the excitement is about to begin."

Desiree smiled back at her friend. "You really love this, don't you?"

Zulu answered the question by grinning even wider, then turned his attention to his area of responsibility.

Track determined that the pirates' Bertram Special Sport Fisherman was within range. He swung the barrel of the Vickers in that direction and kicked off a long stream of bullets. He monitored the tracers as he lowered his aim until able to see the flaming slugs strike the hull of the boat.

A sudden explosion in the water beside the *Fancy Free* heralded the Bertram's antitank gun in action, returning fire. They weren't going to take anything sitting down.

Sir Abner yelled at George. "Let's give them a rocket, lad."

"Right!"

The Englishman veered slightly to port, then suddenly went full in that direction. George brought out the PZF44 and fired. The rocket streaked out, passing so close to the Bertram's flying bridge that the gunners there were forced to duck.

"Damn!" George cursed in frustration as the projectile exploded far on the other side of the target.

Sir Abner quickly got back on course. By presenting their side to the enemy, he was making it easy for the pirates to hit them. He could only maintain a good firing position for George for a couple of minutes at the extreme maximum.

Track, on the other hand, with the wide field of fire he enjoyed with the Vickers, could have numerous targets of opportunity as long as the bad guys didn't get too far ahead of them.

He hosed the Bertram one more time, then swung the machine gun toward the Hatteras Motor Launch. His shots were a bit high.

Track had just started to lower the barrel when the other boat's quad-fifty machine gun opened up. Slugs slammed into the *Fancy Free*, crashing and whining as ricochets zinged off into the tropical air.

Sir Abner quickly assessed the situation and pulled back on the throttles, forcing the Hatteras to get a bit ahead of them.

George saw an opportunity. He swung the tube of the rocket launcher at the pirate and pulled back on the trigger.

An explosive geyser of water showed a near miss. The buccaneer veered off.

The Bertram pumped several more 57 mm shells their way. Two of the rounds hit the flying bridge almost simultaneously, making the *Fancy Free* suddenly list so far that her starboard gunwales were submerged. The sturdy vessel righted herself, but Sir Abner had been flung violently to the deck.

The valiant old ex-commando, his head badly gashed, struggled gamely to get back on his feet, but dizziness caused him to slip and fall again. Once more, with grim determination driving him on, he crawled to the control console and reached up to pull himself to his feet. His hand accidentally hit the starboard throttle, pulling it to Slow Speed.

The port engine, still running fast, pushed the vessel around quickly, forcing it into an uncontrolled tight circle. Sir Abner, experiencing extreme vertigo from his head wound and the motion of the boat, once again collapsed to the deck.

Track was on his knees, hanging on to the firing handles of the Vickers. "Goddamn it!" he yelled toward the helm. "What the hell's going on, Sir Abner?"

The *Fancy Free* shook under a fresh fusillade from the quad-fifty. Bullets pockmarked the afterdeck salon overhead. A shower of splinters and dust filled the compartment.

A trio of sharp explosions from the other pirate vessel's antitank gun ripped at the portside deck. George Beegh did his best to bring the rocket launcher into play, but the violent motion of the boat had flung him hard across one side of the forepeak, and the centrifugal force held him against the bulkhead.

Desiree and Zulu could do nothing but hold on as the vessel continued its rapid rotation.

Track finally let go of the machine gun's handles and slid across the deck to the starboard side. He laboriously began to crawl across the listing expanse toward the door leading to the main cabin. It took him several minutes to reach the opening. He looked in and saw Sir Abner, obviously dazed, feebly trying to reach the control console. The Englishman's face was a mask of blood.

Track, fighting hard against the increased angle of the circling boat, pulled himself into the cabin. Sir Abner, recovering a bit, could see his friend through the red haze of blood on his face.

"I say, Dan," he said calmly. "Would you be so kind as to give us a hand?"

"Glad to," Track said, grimacing. He reached the control console. It took him several minutes, but he managed to get his hand on the starboard throttle. Track strained as he edged the knob forward. The *Fancy Free* gradually straightened out and Track was able to haul himself to his feet and take full control.

The relief they felt lasted only a split second.

Fifty-caliber machine gun slugs and 57 mm shells raked the vessel, engulfing it in a hailstorm of roaring steel. Track, knowing the pirate Hatteras was a bit slower than the Bertram, turned boldly toward it, presenting a smaller target.

Sir Abner joined him at the wheel. "I'll take it now, old son."

"Sure you can handle it?" Track asked.

"Of course!"

"Okay," Track said. "Give me a minute to get back to the Vickers, then spin this baby on her heels and get me a good sight picture on that Hatteras."

"Go for it, as you Yanks say."

Track raced back to the machine gun and braced himself. The *Fancy Free*, under Sir Abner's quick manipulation of wheel and throttles, spun a U-turn, presenting its bow to the Hatteras's port side.

Track, trusting in the water-cooling mechanism to keep the barrels from burning out, pressed the trigger on the Vickers. He allowed a continuous stream of .303 slugs to rake the enemy vessel.

The onslaught was too much for the pirate. He quickly broke contact and drew off. With his companion outmaneuvered, the firing quickly stopped.

"Dan, old son!" Sir Abner called. "I've a bit of an idea."

Track, with a chance to leave the gun for a moment, joined the Englishman in the cabin. "What's up, Sir Abner?"

"We're in a bit of a jam, what?"

"We're shook up and outgunned," Track admitted.

"I should think this is an opportune time for a desperate ploy," Sir Abner said. "We're not quite at a point of 'all or nothing,' but we're damned close."

"You're right," Track said. "What's this idea of yours?"

"I'm going to 'cross the T,'" the Englishman said.

Track thought for a moment. "If I recall correctly, that means allowing the broad beam of the enemy ship to go across our bow while we rake it with fire, right?"

"Right," Sir Abner said. "But the only effective weapon we have to the front is George's rocket launcher. Which means if he fires directly forward, the backblast will blow me, the control console and most of the *Fancy Free* directly to hell."

"So how are you going to 'cross the T'?" Track asked.

"The hard way, old boy, by the stern," Sir Abner said.

"You mean go at 'em backward?"

"That's the way. With you and that Vickers giving them a jolly good hosing, what?"

Track shrugged. "What the hell? We're getting knocked ass over teakettle now, anyhow. Let's go for it."

"Right. But one thing first."

"Sure," Track said. "What do you need?"

"Would you get a bandage from the first-aid kit, old boy, and put it around my head?" Sir Abner asked. "The blood keeps getting into my eyes."

With Sir Abner tightly bandaged, Track quickly went to each battle station to brief the others on the planned maneuver.

The pirates had managed to arrange themselves into an attack formation, and the two vessels roared in at the solitary *Fancy Free*.

Sir Abner wasted no time. He headed directly toward the Bertram, the closest target. By concentrating on the one vessel, the *Fancy Free* would be farther away from the Hatteras.

Sir Abner had both throttles wide open. He slashed through the waves directly toward the Bertram. The pirate's antitank gun fired rapidly. Watery explosions erupted on both sides of the *Fancy Free*.

"Get ready, Dan!" Sir Abner called.

He swung their boat off to port, momentarily making her a broad target. The pirate gunners were good. They saw their opportunity and began to increase their efforts.

Then Sir Abner executed one of his precise U-turns with the starboard throttle going full bore, the port throttle off and the wheel cranked all the way in that direction.

The *Fancy Free* zipped quickly around.

Track found his target off to his left a bit, but it "crossed the T" beautifully. He was able to completely rake the Bertram with a long, steady stream of slugs. The enemy vessel shuddered under the uninterrupted volley. Several tracers hit the flying bridge, going into the antitank gun's ammo.

The explosion was truly remarkable.

The vessel was there one moment, then suddenly it was engulfed in a brilliant orange cloud that seemed to suck in the air around it. An instant later, there was nothing to be seen but a mutilated hull sinking quickly beneath the waves.

Desiree and Zulu, cheering, joined Track in the afterdeck salon. "One down and one to go!" Track yelled. He rushed to the main cabin. "Shall we try it with the other?"

Sir Abner's bloody face was grim. He spun the wheel. It gyrated wildly on its hub, but the *Fancy Free* continued on a relatively straight course. "That great explosion caused a tremendous underwater concussion," Sir Abner said. "Our rudders are gone!"

Track quickly joined him. He worked the wheel back and forth, but the sturdy vessel failed to respond.

Sir Abner looked at his friend. "Our lovely *Fancy Free*, from this point on, will follow only those courses set by the fickle fates."

Track started to reply, but he looked out at the ocean around them. "Oh, shit!" he suddenly yelled. "Here comes that fucking Hatteras with the quad-fifties!"

Sir Abner shoved both throttles to Full Speed and flung himself on the deck to join the others. The *Fancy Free* leaped forward, picking up unguided speed across the open ocean.

Then first rounds from the enemy's machine guns slammed into the valiant *Fancy Free*, the impact beginning the job of shaking her to bits.

17

The world had turned into a hell of exploding slugs, screaming ricochets and splintering wood.

The *Fancy Free*, as brave a vessel as ever sailed on the dangerous Spanish Main, shuddered and rolled under the onslaught of steel-jacketed slugs. Rudderless, but with both diesel engines thundering ahead on full speed, she ploughed her bow into the waves while the merciless killer off her port stern blasted round after round of heavy machine gun bullets into the courageous boat.

Track, flat on his belly with the others, let out an enraged bellow. "If I'm gonna die, goddamn it, I'll do it on my feet!" He leaped up and raced to the Vickers. He swung the gun over to his right and lay down heavily on the trigger.

Shrieking slugs and debris flew around his head as he sprayed the pirate back with flashing tracers and hot lead. The Hatteras, taking serious hits, tried an evasive action by swinging over to the opposite side. But Track, thanks to the design of the afterdeck salon's gun position, was able to move with the pursuing boat. The pirate, taking too many hits, dropped back out of range.

Suddenly the Vickers stopped firing.

"What the fuck!" Track yelled in frustrated rage.

"You need another belt!" George yelled. He rushed to the machine gun's side and reached inside the ammunition box, but it was empty. He looked frantically around. "Where's the rest of the ammo?"

"In the stowage locker," Track said.

George rushed below decks for more.

"Goddamn me for an idiot!" Track cursed himself. "I should've kept a closer eye on my supply."

"Under the circumstances I think you've made a damned good job of it," Sir Abner said.

Desiree glanced up. "Here he comes again."

"Hurry, George!" Zulu yelled.

The Hatteras, quad-fifty blasting, closed in. Once more the interior of the *Fancy Free* became an exploding, roaring hell as it shook and quaked under the pounding of the .50-caliber slugs.

George appeared in the hatchway with a heavy box of .303 ammunition in each hand. He ignored the thundering danger and rushed to the gun. Track opened the breech as George quickly inserted a belt. "Way to go," Track said, cranking the charging handle.

He pulled up the barrel to shoot, but suddenly the flying bridge above them crashed down, blocking his field of fire. Zulu hurried into the main cabin to the firefighting kit and returned with the ax. His muscles rippled and bulged with the physical effort as he chopped at the large hunk of debris.

All this time the incoming volley never let up. The only effect it had on the brave black man was to make him turn his head away when splinters flew up into his face. Within ten minutes he'd cleared the wreckage and, with everyone helping, pushed it overboard.

The stern of the *Fancy Free* was wide open now and there was no overhead in the afterdeck salon. Track appreciated the more open field of fire it now gave him. He swung the Vickers into action and managed to fire off a long burst of a dozen rounds when suddenly flames flashed up on the stern.

The *Fancy Free*'s forward motion stopped.

"The engines!" Sir Abner yelled. "They've hit them!"

George crawled rearward for a look. He hurried back as black, oily smoke bellowed upward. "The fuel tanks are burning, Dan! We're on fire!"

The pirate vessel, hidden in the thick, rolling smoke, moved in for the final—killing—run.

Track, completely blinded by the conflagration, let go of the Vickers. He walked over to the settee and slumped down.

"Shit!" he said. "We've had it."

The first rounds of the fresh fusillade slammed into the *Fancy Free*.

PABLO ORTIZ STOOD in front of the counter in Stubby Boudreaux's chandlery. He was ill at ease, but fought to keep a friendly smile on his face.

Stubby, on the other side, slowly pulled a packet of Red Chief chewing tobacco from his pocket. Without speaking, he took a wad of the stuff and stuck it in his mouth.

Pablo's uneasiness grew in the silence. "Listen, Stubby, you got no call for to be pissed off on me, eh?"

"Maybe I do," Stubby allowed, "maybe I don't."

"I din't have nothing to di wit' Dinkum and Darby beatin' on you, man," Pablo said. "I'm just a security guy."

Several gunsels had shown up, and there was some remodeling going on of the marina since Mr. Banks had given Stubby Pedro's old job. Pablo, now unemployed because of the reorganization, had come down from Hobart to see if there was a place for him. Stubby shifted the chaw. "Why should I hire you?"

"We've known each other a long time, man," Pablo said. "And if somebody oughta be pissed off, it's me, right? I mean, Marvin Leroy really clouted me in the alley the night you offed Pedro, man! But I ain't mad."

Stubby reached across the bar and grabbed the larger man by the collar and pulled him down to his fat face. "You listen to me, goddamn you! What makes you think I'd hire you for a guard? I went through you to git at yore boss. You think I want you takin' care o' things around here?"

"So I fucked up once, man," Pablo said, pulling himself free of the other man's pudgy fist. "You gringos got a sayin' 'bout bein' once burned, twice shy, right?"

"Well—maybe we do."

"I'll be a good man for you, Stubby. No shit."

"Okay," Stubby said. "I'll hire you on one condition."

"Sure, man!" Pablo said happily. "Name it, man!"

"You gotta fight Marvin Leroy."

Pablo's olive complexion paled, and he swallowed hard. "That Marvin Leroy is pretty *grandote*—big!"

"You listen to me, you sumbitch," Stubby said. "You fight him and I'll give you a job."

Pablo pondered the proposition for a minute. "Do I got to win?"

Stubby shook his head. "Nope."

"Okay. I fight the big kid, then."

"Right now?" Stubby asked.

Pablo sighed. "Sure. Why not?"

Stubby laughed. "You're hired, you sumbitch! If'n you got the guts to go up against a big bastard like ol' Marvin Leroy, then I know yo're bad enough to be one o' my boys."

Pablo grinned in relief. He was sincerely, eternally grateful. "Hey, thanks a lot, Stubby. You won't be sorry.

If some *hijo de la chingada* comes around here, I'll waste him for you fast.''

Stubby knew he had just won over a loyal subject. ''C'mon, Pablo. I'll show you around the place and explain the operation to you.''

Pablo took the invitation to walk around the counter and go into the back room of the chandlery. Stubby's usual merchandise was there, but there had been some additions. Beyond the shelves of food and boat supplies was another room recently added on. It, too, was for storage, but the items here would definitely not be for normal commercial use.

A large trapdoor was located in the middle of the room. Stubby bent over and opened it. ''This here's both shippin' and receivin'.''

Pablo peered down the opening and could see a freshly made floating dock large enough to accommodate a boat up to forty-five feet in length. The Cuban whisled in admiration. ''Looks like they got you set up good, Stubby.''

''You bet,'' Stubby said. He pointed upward. ''See the hoist there? That baby'll handle up to two tons in one swoop. We'll unload fast, and then the next boat comes along we'll load her up just as fast.''

''You gonna go from one boat to another?''

''Yeah,'' Stubby explained. ''The guys bringin' in the goods will just stay long enough to drop their stuff. Then, when the time's right, we'll put it aboard a safe boat that's well-known around here so it won't attract no special attention. That dude'll drop it off somewheres else.''

''Are we still gonna set up boats to be grabbed out at sea like before?''

''Yeah,'' Stubby said. ''And now it'll be faster. I won't have to go through a third person no more. That way the guys out there can get 'em quicker.''

''A sweet setup, man,'' Pablo said.

"Yeah," Stubby agreed. "And we got this place secured, too. That'll be part o' yore job."

"Standin' guard?" Pablo asked.

"There's more to it than that," Stubby said. "Mr. Banks is puttin' in all kinds o' electric gear—radar and whatnot. He's got a coupla boys up there at the ol' boathouse that listen in on the U.S. of A. Coast Guard and the Customs boys, too."

"It'll take a genius *grande* to bust in here," Pablo said.

"Yeah," Stubby said, "either that or a real pissed-off sumbitch."

"Them's the guys you got to look out for," Pablo said.

Stubby laughed, then took him back to the front of the chandlery.

"ELLES SONT FINIES, LES MUNITIONS?" Matamore asked incredulously.

The machine gunner, dirty and sweat streaked, shrugged. "I'm afraid so, *chef*. We are out of ammunition."

Captain Leroux turned his chubby countenance to look at the *Fancy Free*. She was still in the water just out of range. He caught sight of the two men foaming her burning engines with fire extinguishers. "They cannot get under way," he remarked. "If only we could close in on them."

"We will board them," Matamore said.

Leroux shook his head. "They still have their machine gun, *chef*. And they have a rocket launcher to the front. We'd never get close enough."

Matamore's voice was cold. "It was not a request, *capitaine*. It was an order."

The machine gunner shook his head. "Leroux is right, *chef*. It would be a suicide run."

Matamore pulled his .45 and instantly swung it up into the gunner's face. The pistol kicked back in recoil, and the man's head jerked back and his legs collapsed a second before he fell to the deck.

The helmsman turned at the sound of the shot, then immediately and fearfully focused his attention back on his duties. Leroux's expression showed shock and alarm. He looked at Matamore.

Matamore calmly repeated himself. "I gave an order."

Leroux nodded. *"Mais oui, chef."* He walked over to the hatch leading below decks. "Everyone report to the main cabin, *vite*!" he shouted.

Matamore stepped back to a corner, holding the pistol ready for instant use. Within moments the remainder of the crew crowded in through the door. They stared down at the dead gunner.

"The quad-fifty has no bullets left," Leroux announced. "So we are going to close in on the enemy boat and board her."

If any of the men disagreed with the idea, they kept it to themselves. There was an excellent object lesson sprawled on the deck at their feet.

"Position yourselves along the portside deck," Leroux ordered. "As soon as we close with the other boat, leap aboard."

The men started to check their sidearms, but Matamore cautioned them. "If your weapons are not ready, you will pay the price for your inattention."

There was a brief, low muttering as the crew went to their positions. One suddenly whirled around, with a quickly drawn revolver in his hand.

Matamore instantly dropped to a crouch, holding his automatic straight out in both hands. He pulled the trigger twice, each bullet striking home on the challenger. The sailor, grimacing from the shock of the two hits, was propelled backward by the impact. He hit the rail on the side deck and flipped backward over into the sea.

"Any more questions or expressions of displeasure or disagreement?" Matamore asked.

Leroux silently marveled at the man. Not only did he hold a half dozen armed thugs at bay, but he was forcing them into a suicide mission against a heavy machine gun!

"Allez!" Matamore ordered.

The helmsman hit the throttles and the Hatteras quickly picked up speed. Within fifteen minutes they were close enough to the *Fancy Free* to see the tracers zipping at them from the wild gunner who manned the weapon.

Slugs began cracking into the boat, their intensity gradually increasing until it sounded like a gigantic swarm of steel hornets. Bits of glass, plastic and wood spun through the air.

A couple of crewmen were slammed off the boat. One pirate, badly hit, staggered inside the cabin with an arm nearly blown off. Another leaped into the sea, preferring to take his chances with the sharks.

Leroux found his courage.

"Merde de merde!" he yelled. "We will gain nothing by this!"

Matamore, finally regaining his sanity, nodded. "Pull away! We will return to Ile-a-Salut and reoutfit for another try at the *diable de bateau*!"

The helmsman, hearing the order, quickly turned out of the steel storm and gunned the motor to speed them to a safer area.

Leroux sighed in relief. He looked at Matamore. *"Diable de bateau* you called her, eh? Well, *chef*, you are right. She is, indeed, a devil boat!"

"And I shall cast her back into hell!" Matamore snarled.

18

Kiowa O'Keefe, trying to home in on the loudest signal, purposely yawed the Catalina Flying Boat as the beeps in the earphones increased in intensity. These came from the old fashioned radio-navigation gear of his ancient aircraft. As soon as he was satisfied he was locked in on the proper azimuth leading to the *Fancy Free*, he used wheel and rudder to get on the correct course.

It was midmorning on a beautiful day. The sky was a deep but bright blue and the Caribbean Sea glistened almost turquoise. The water was so clear and shallow in some spots that O'Keefe could spot large sea creatures during brief glances through the window of his airplane.

Finally, three-quarters of an hour out of Kingston, the signals from the radio-navigation set were so loud that he knew he would be able to make visual contact soon. O'Keefe pulled back on the control column and climbed another thousand feet. He banked the wings and began making a wide, lazy circle as he scanned the watery expanse below for a sighting of his quarry.

After ten minutes of looking, he spotted the white object bobbing in the ocean. He eased into a gentle dive, then leveled off at less than five hundred feet and zoomed over the boat.

It was the *Fancy Free*, no doubt. He recognized the crew—but certainly not the boat. Badly beaten up, with its stern a blackened jumble and a gaping hole where the

flying bridge had been, the vessel was a mess. The five
people aboard her, however, seemed to be in excellent
spirits. They waved enthusiastically at him.

O'Keefe came in easily on the glass-smooth sea, instantly throttling back as he approached the boat. Closer
observation told him that it was powerless. The vessel
drifted aimlessly with the current and what little wind there
was. He taxied through the water until one giant wing was
directly over the damaged craft. Then he quickly cut the
engines.

On board the *Fancy Free*, Zulu and George quickly
opened the side viewing port of the airplane and leaped
inside. Track and Sir Abner threw them lines that were
immediately secured to the stowage rings of the big flying
machine.

Kiowa O'Keefe left the cockpit and walked back into the
fuselage. He was attired, as usual, in an old orange U.S.
Navy flying suit, cowboy boots and Stetson. He grinned a
casual greeting. "Howdy."

George, who had just looped a line through a tie-down
ring, gave a wave. "How're you doing, Kiowa?"

"A lot better'n you folks evidently," O'Keefe said,
looking outside at the badly damaged boat. "It appears to
me like you showed up at an ax free-for-all without an ax!"

"It was almost that bad," Zulu said. He glanced around
the crowded fuselage. "I'm rather surprised to see this extra gear. Sir Abner had said he'd requested that we be
picked up and flown back to Jamaica."

"Right," O'Keefe said. "But I've got some news for you
that might change your plans. Can we talk aboard what's
left of your boat, or is everybody coming over here?"

"Our refrigeration is gone, and the only thing we have
to offer you is some rather tepid water," Zulu said.

"Don't worry," O'Keefe said with a laugh. "Behind
those boxes over there are a half dozen cases of iced beer."

"As Sir Abner would say, 'You're a gentleman of the highest order,'" George said.

"A veritable godsend!" Zulu exclaimed.

"Let's get it aboard," George said.

Within fifteen minutes, enjoying the taste of the cold brew, Track and Company were hosting their guest aboard the burned-out hulk of the *Fancy Free*. There was shade of sorts from the remainder of the flying bridge. Sir Abner, his head freshly and neatly bandaged by Desiree, had almost recovered fully from the injury. A dull ache, which he completely ignored, was the principal remaining symptom.

Dan Track tipped his head back and chugalugged a bottle of beer. Then he tossed the empty to the deck and emitted a long, satisfying belch. "That," he said in an understatement, "tasted good."

"Want another?" O'Keefe asked.

"You bet," Track said. He took a second beer from the pilot. "I've been meaning to ask you something, Kiowa."

"What's that?"

"If you're half Irish and half Scottish like you say, why is your first name Kiowa? Isn't that an Indian name, or is it a nickname?"

"It's actually a tribe of Plains Indians," Kiowa conceded. "But it's also my real name. But I wasn't named after those particular Native Americans. I'm from Kiowa County, Oklahoma. My people have lived there since the turn of the century when the area was first opened for settlement. Since the place had been so good to us for a couple of generations, my father thought it would be fitting and proper to name his first son after the county. So, here's a straw-haired, blue-eyed boy named Kiowa."

"Your county, hey?" Track remarked. "How about that?"

O'Keefe laughed aloud. "I'm just happy as hell I wasn't born in Pottawatomie County!"

Sir Abner chuckled and sipped from his own bottle of beer. "I say, Kiowa, how does a lad from Oklahoma end up flying a vintage seaplane over the Spanish Main?"

"That, my friends, isn't really much of a story," Kiowa O'Keefe said. "I entered the navy's pilot-training program after I graduated from Oklahoma State. I didn't make jet jockey, but I did get a lot of carrier flying in various types of multiengine radar aircraft."

Track interjected. "I remember meeting some Air Force pilots in an officers' club during my Army days. They were discussing a liaison tour they'd made with the Navy. Those flyboys described carrier landings as controlled crashes."

"Hell! We were better than that," O'Keefe said. "Anyhow, I'm kind of an individualist and military life rubbed me raw in certain ways. When my Navy term of service was over, a contact I'd made got me a chance to fly for a small cargo carrier out of Miami, Florida."

George Beegh popped open another bottle. "That sounds like a good job."

"It was boring as an old ladies' quilting bee," O'Keefe said. "So I decided to go into business for myself when I found out about this Catalina for sale. It sounded sort of romantic and adventurous, you know. Island hopping and all that stuff."

"Have your efforts been successful?" Desiree asked.

"I'm making a pretty good living," O'Keefe answered. "But I'm afraid it's a rather dull existence, too."

"Except when you fly for The Consortium, huh?" Track asked.

"I'll admit to a couple of interesting experiences," O'Keefe said with a wink. "But I'm sworn to secrecy."

"I happen to know you're completely trustworthy and enjoy a great deal of confidence," Sir Abner said. "My closest associates in The Consortium have assured me on that point."

"That reminds me," O'Keefe said. He reached into his flying suit and brought out a manila envelope. "This is for you, Sir Abner."

Sir Abner opened the package and pulled several sheets of paper from it. "I say! It's not in code."

O'Keefe winked at him. "Like you said—they trust me."

"I should think so!" Sir Abner exclaimed. "Please excuse me. I must peruse these documents."

It took the Englishman fifteen minutes to carefully read the information. When he finished, he looked at Kiowa O'Keefe. "Is that why you've brought the extra equipment?"

"Yes, sir," O'Keefe answered.

"What's up?" Track wanted to know.

"This is intelligence on the origin of our pirates," Sir Abner said. "One of The Consortium contacts came through with some information from a rather disgruntled young lady in Colon, Panama. She was angry over the death of a lover. She blamed it on the man running the boat-stealing show."

"Sounds like a reliable source," Track said.

"No doubt," Desiree mused aloud. "We women have a tendency to get upset when our men get killed."

"What sort of information did she pass on?" Zulu asked.

"It seems they're from an island off Haiti called Ile-a-Salut. Here's a map."

Track took the topographical printout and studied it quickly. "Heavy jungle all around except for the harbor there," he noted. "Looks like a great place for an invasion."

George glanced up at his uncle. "Got something in mind, Dan?"

Track, lost in thought, didn't answer.

Zulu nodded his head. "He has something in mind—most definitely!"

MADELEINE NOIRE WAS PRESSED hard against the bed as Philippe possessed her body with violent, surging thrusts. There was more anger than passion in his lovemaking, and he seemed insatiable.

Finally Matamore reached a climax, grinding farther into her with a low growl of masculine pleasure. Madeleine, a bit frightened, felt him relax and soften inside her. Then he withdrew, leaving her spent and exhausted, breathing so heavily that it sounded as if she were sobbing.

Madeleine had known something was terribly wrong when she'd first sighted him from the veranda. Matamore had come from the harbor up to the mansion with angry, long strides. As he drew closer she could see the cuts on his face and the blood that had flowed down onto the tank top he wore.

She had called out to him, but he'd not acknowledged her greeting. Instead, Matamore had ascended the steps and grabbed her hand, pulling her through the large house to their bedroom.

Her original plan to seductively disrobe in a slow, provocative strip had been ripped aside like her clothes. Madeleine was picked up bodily and flung on the bed. Then the man, his own clothes hastily removed, had mounted her in a frenzy of fury, venting his anger and frustration on her like a stallion taming a defiant mare.

Matamore left her there, going into the bathroom. As Madeleine sat up she could hear the shower running. She noticed bruises along the inside of her thighs. Madeleine got to her feet and retrieved her scattered clothing. After a close inspection of the garments, she threw them to the floor. All had been ripped apart.

Naked, she walked across the bedroom to the dresser and pulled out a halter and shorts. By the time she'd finished dressing, Matamore rejoined her. He toweled off his long, muscular body without speaking.

"Chéri?" Madeleine said softly.

Matamore ignored her. He went to the closet and pulled out a fresh suit and shirt. When he had finished dressing, he strapped on a shoulder holster. He settled the .45 auto in it and walked out onto the veranda.

Madeleine hurried to the fridge and joined him outside, handing him a frosted mug filled with Miragoane Beer. He took it without acknowledging her, drinking long and deep.

A knock on the door startled her. *"Que voulez-vous?"*

"I wish to speak with *el jefe.*" It was the voice of the radio operator.

Matamore drew the pistol and turned toward the door. "Come in."

The man stepped into the room and halted, staring wide-eyed at the gun. He smiled uneasily. "Some of the men want to see you, *jefe.* They are on the back porch."

Matamore strode past Madeleine and the caller, walking rapidly down the hall and out the door of the mansion. Several men stood at the head of the steps. From their expressions, he could tell they were angry. He raised the pistol and began firing.

Two dropped down the steps immediately. The others quickly turned and fled. Matamore fired again, dropping another man, who crawled away clutching his wounded leg.

A noise off to the side of the house caught Matamore's attention. He rushed to that end of the porch in time to see the radio operator disappear into the thick jungle growth. Matamore wasted a shot at the fleeing man. Seething with anger, he sensed someone behind him. Holding the pistol, he whirled.

It was Madeleine standing fearlessly in the front door. She looked at him boldly, then a slight smile played across her lips.

"I am your woman."

Matamore lowered the pistol.

"ANY PARTICULAR PLAN of action?" George asked Track.

"According to the intelligence report, the head of the outfit is a coldhearted son of a bitch named Philippe Matamore," Track said. "A tall, slim black man."

"Any photos?" Desiree asked.

"Unfortunately, no," Track answered. "There's only a brief description and a bit of information about his service in the Tonton Macoutes."

"The bogeymen," Zulu remarked. "The Haitian Secret Police. No wonder there are no photographic portraits of Monsieur Matamore."

"Right," Sir Abner said, with the report in his lap. "The source identified him as the heart and soul of the operation. Remove him and it will take them months to renew their buccaneer activities."

Track laid a finger at a point on the map. "This is where he lives." He studied the layout again. "Damn! Getting into that harbor and through the village to reach him would be impossible."

Sir Abner was thoughtful for a few moments. "Of course we could do as the Japanese did to our chaps at Singapore."

Track looked up. "How was that?"

"Well, all the British guns were pointed to the sea," Sir Abner explained. "And the place was a veritable bastion.

If the Japanese stormed it, they would have suffered horrible casualties and still not be guaranteed a success."

George was interested. "So what did they do?"

"They came in through the back door, old boy," Sir Abner said. "The little bastards hacked their way through the jungle and damned near just walked in. The point is, the unexpected won in that case."

Track looked at the map again. "If we could come in through the jungle there, we could hit that big house from the back without anyone seeing us."

Zulu, looking over his shoulder, nodded. "Right. It would be tough going, though. And how should we get there?"

Kiowa O'Keefe cleared his throat. "Ahem! I happen to have a mode of transportation quite handy." He pointed to the large airplane beside the *Fancy Free*.

"We'd have to go in daylight, and they would hear us," Track said.

"There's plenty of air traffic through that area," O'Keefe told him. "The sound of an aircraft's motors wouldn't attract any undue attention, and, anyway, I could set down in the water out of sight of the inhabited part of the island. Hell, I have a one-man raft in there you could use to carry your weapons and other gear in on."

Desiree took Track's beer and sipped from it. "A good infiltration method, but it will not be very effective for exfiltration."

"We'll have the element of surprise with us," Track said. "We pull the hit, then charge into the harbor and get a boat to get us out of there."

"But we'll be pursued by other vessels," Sir Abner argued. "How can we be guaranteed an escape?"

"Ahem!" Kiowa O'Keefe again cleared his throat. "I'll meet you folks any place you want."

Track took his beer back from Desiree and drained it. He tossed the bottle across what was left of the afterdeck salon. "Okay," he said. "Let's firm it up."

19

The code words "Jolly Roger" had been broadcast by Kiowa O'Keefe over his aircraft radio on the frequency utilized by The Consortium. This, according to the instructions in the manila envelope sent to Sir Abner Chesterton, would alert The Consortium's representative that an attack on the pirates' lair would be forthcoming. There were actions this individual would take, but the message to the Englishman had not specified exactly what these would be.

It was obvious The Consortium's agent in attendance was expecting some sort of action. He had included a special crate of apparel and equipment suitable for operation in jungle terrain. Tropical boots, lightweight fatigues, canteens and other gear were available for Track and Company.

They managed to pack needed equipment from the *Fancy Free* onto the aircraft. Personal weapons, clothing, George's tried and true PZF44 Rocket launcher, a few rockets, grenades and other miscellaneous paraphernalia were loaded on.

Since the Vickers heavy machine gun wasn't an essential part of any future plans, it was left aboard. The unfired ammunition for the weapon and its tool kit were also abandoned. It seemed a terrible waste, but there was no choice. Kiowa O'Keefe's old airplane would have enough trouble straining itself off the water into the air without the extra burden of weight.

Then the saddest task of all had to be taken care of.

Rather than let the *Fancy Free* drift as a derelict, it was decided to give the noble lady a dignified send-off. Five incendiary grenades were taken below decks to scuttle her.

Track and Company had gone to do the job together. Then, in an unspoken and unplanned ceremony, each pulled the pin from a grenade and gently set down the deadly canister.

Within ten seconds, after the crew had left her, the thermite TH3 mixture was burning at a temperature of nearly four thousand degrees Fahrenheit. These fiery bits of hell were capable of burning through a half inch of homogeneous armor plating.

After they were set off, all hands reboarded the Catalina. O'Keefe pulled off a way, and the crew turned to bid their last goodbye to a vessel that had taken plenty of hits but had given back a hell of a lot more. The grenades, AMM14 TH3s, produced their own oxygen and therefore would burn even underwater.

The lady died in dignity.

Sinking slowly, gracefully, the *Fancy Free* slipped beneath the waves to settle on the bottom. A braver craft had never sailed the Spanish Main.

Sir Abner and Zulu, standing side by side in the fuselage, suddenly and instinctively assumed positions of attention and snapped salutes.

Desiree Goth wept quietly and proudly.

Both Track and George Beegh threw American equivalents of a high ball.

Then O'Keefe revved the engines and began the taxi for takeoff. After gaining a few hundred feet of altitude, he made one pass over the spot where the gallant lady had made her farewell. Then, with the proper course set on the autopilot and the throttles open, he headed for their destination.

It was high noon on the uninhabited side of Ile-a-Salut when O'Keefe lowered the flaps and brought his Catalina in for a splashy landing less than a hundred yards off the island. Track, Zulu, George and Desiree, all clad in bathing suits, leaped into the sea. The old commando would not be going with them. While his head wound was not giving him serious problems, it was a potential cause of trouble and delay. They all felt the risk was too great, and he reluctantly agreed with his comrades at arms.

O'Keefe and Sir Abner pushed the small rubber raft out to the raiders, then passed out the various weapons, ammo and clothing they would require for their mission.

Track had estimated that if they hit the beach around midday, they would be able to get through the jungle and make the hit on the mansion in the late afternoon. That would give them time to get to the harbor and head for the open ocean to meet O'Keefe and his plane at the approximate time the rapid tropical dusk would be descending on the area.

Thus, with all aboard, the Catalina would be climbing into a dark sky for the final flight to Kingston and safety.

Now, swimming and pushing the raft, the quartet of invaders made their way toward the short expanse of narrow beach. George, spitting out seawater, said, "This is getting to be a habit with us, huh?"

"What's that?" Track asked.

"Making invasions by water," he said. "Remember the strike against that son of a bitch Levant out in California?"

"Not quite the same," Zulu reminded him. "As I recall we were quite dry when we stepped out on the beach."

It took them less than fifteen minutes to reach land. Once there, they hurriedly dragged the raft into the nearby jungle. Dressing quickly, they grabbed their gear and began the slow journey through the dense vegetation.

The going was rough. The heat immediately pressed down on them in the green hell like a heavy blanket of steam. They perspired in energy-sapping streams, and the sweat would not evaporate in the high humidity. Instead it only added to their physical discomfort.

Vines, branches and brush seemed to reach out and grab at them, slowing them down and making each yard traveled a frustrating fight. Insects soon discovered their presence and descended on the raiding team with a vengeance. Biting and buzzing maddeningly in their ears, noses and mouths, the swarming bugs stung in angry frenzy.

After two hours, Track, in the lead, could sense the low ebb of morale and the fraying tempers. He looked back at them. Little flying creatures buzzed around their eyes, and sweat beaded on their dirty faces and cascaded down to their filthy fatigues in salty, burning rivulets. He wet his lips and spoke to his team.

"I wonder what the poor folks are doing today?"

MADELEINE NOIRE was from *le peuple des cannes à sucre*—sugarcane people. Poverty-stricken and volatile, they had little going for them but their personal pride and courage. And they backed these up with the same tools they used to make their living—machetes.

With her man now under threat, Madeleine had gotten her hands on a machete and kept it under their bed. The cutting instrument, as sharp as a surgeon's scalpel, had been used by the workman who kept the incessant jungle growth away from the old plantation house.

If anyone came near Philippe Matamore or Madeleine Noire, he would be forced to deal with that machete and the woman who could wield it so skilfully.

The hamlet on Ile-a-Salut was in chaos.

While Matamore had faced no head-on challenges, his authority was now in serious question. The return of the badly damaged Hatteras with the news of the loss of so many more men and both the Magnum speedboat and the Bertram Sport had set the dope smugglers' teeth on edge.

They were mad as hell, and someone was going to pay for it.

TRACK SIGNALED a halt.

His companions quickly ceased movement. Then he stepped carefully through the brush, making sure to keep any loud rustling of vegetation to an absolute minimum.

At the edge of the jungle he stopped. The old plantation house was directly in front of him. He noted the strangeness of the structure's appearance. Parts, particularly on the south side where the rotted siding and paneless windows were covered with thick vines, seemed ready to collapse. Yet there had been some recent remodeling on the north end. A window air conditioner hummed, and there were even curtains visible.

Track's eyes swept the area, noting the absence of guards. He decided to enter the structure through the obviously unused south side.

He pulled back to the others and told them his plan. Track reminded them of the uncertain danger. "This is risky. We don't know the layout of the place."

"Hell!" George said. "We don't even know if that Matamore character is inside or not."

"And if he is," Zulu reminded them, "we shall have to take him and anyone else there out silently."

"If things go to hell, we'll have to make a fighting run for it to the harbor," Track said. "The odds aren't good at all."

Desiree smiled. "They never are for us, darling."

George grinned and patted Track on the face. "That's right, dear."

"Get screwed, asshole!" Track said, laughing. "Let's go."

They stayed at the jungle's edge for as long as possible. Then all poised themselves. On Track's signal, the group ran across the small open space between the vegetation and the house, entering the structure's doorless south entrance.

Desiree glanced around at the filthy interior. She could see past its decay, her imagination enabling her to picture the grandeur that had once dominated the place. "Elegant people lived here at one time," she whispered.

Zulu nodded. "Yes, Desiree. There are ghosts from the old plantation days walking these premises."

"Maybe so," Track said, "but right now there's probably some modern bad asses that need taking care of."

"Let's get to it," George said.

They split into two teams to reconnoiter the old mansion. George and Zulu went down one hall while Track and Desiree entered a kitchen.

There was nothing there but a rusted-out ancient stove and some cabinets that had tumbled down with the passage of time. A large pantry was off to one side. They eased into that and continued on until they reached a set of doors.

"Shall we stick together or save time and each take one?" Track asked.

Desiree shifted her Uzi and answered the question by stepping through the nearest portal. Track took the other.

The young woman found herself in a musty hallway. Heavy green mold encrusted the high ceiling. She continued on until she came to another entrance. Pressing her ear to the door, Desiree listened carefully, then eased it open.

The room before her was a bedroom. It was clean and airy, and a veranda could be seen off to one side. A canopied bed and other furniture showed the chamber was used. Desiree stepped inside.

The blow caught her just behind the ear and she stumbled forward, the Uzi falling to the floor with a clatter. Desiree immediately rolled over and looked up to see a tall, beautiful black woman wearing nothing but panties.

Desiree made a move for the submachine gun, but the woman was faster. She kicked it hard, making it slide under the bed. "Who are you, bitch?"

Desiree got to her feet. "I am not here to harm you."

Madeleine Noire laughed without humor. "You most certainly are not." She eyed Desiree carefully. "Whose woman are you? I have never seen you before."

Desiree sized up the other quickly. Tall, athletic and physically capable, she would be a worthy opponent. "I am my own woman."

"Ha! What cowardly brute sent you to kill my Philippe rather than come himself?" Madeleine Noire demanded.

Desiree immediately recognized the name. "Philippe Matamore?"

"Of course Philippe Matamore!" Madeline snapped. She edged quickly to the bed and reached under the cover. The machete she withdrew glistened in the afternoon sunlight that slanted into the room through the trees outside.

Desiree maintained her cool. She assumed a *fudo dachi* ready stance. Unmoving, outwardly calm but with every muscle poised for instant action, she waited for the larger woman's next move.

Madeleine, who had first chopped cane with a machete at the age of four, made a side swing that whistled through the air.

Desiree hit the woman's arm with a *chudan soto uke*, a middle outer block that stopped the incoming blow cold and quickly.

Any other person might have lost the grip on the weapon, but Madeleine simply tossed it over to her left hand and made a slashing bold assault.

Expecting that style of attack, Desiree quickly shot her hands up and grabbed Madeleine's wrist. She allowed the momentum of the blow to continue, but controlled it as she pivoted and stepped back into the other's body. A quick bend at the waist, and Madeleine flew over Desiree to land flat on the floor.

Now Desiree held the machete.

She waved it at Madeleine. "Stay on the floor, dear."

Madeleine snarled and got to her hands and feet, her large, taut breasts barely swinging.

Desiree was gently persistent. "If you continue this cattiness, I shall have to teach you a most unpleasant woman-to-woman lesson."

A male voice interrupted her. "That won't be necessary."

Philippe Matamore stood in the veranda. A frosted mug of beer was in one hand, and his .45 auto in the other. "Drop the machete." He motioned to Madeleine. "Please step aside, *chérie*."

Madeleine smirked at Desiree as she got to her feet. She blew a kiss to her lover. *"Mais oui, chéri."*

Matamore raised the pistol to take a steady aim. Then he lowered it. "You know," he said thoughtfully. "I have never had a European woman."

Madeleine's eyes snapped his way. "Philippe!"

Matamore waved her away. "Leave the room, Madeleine." He walked slowly toward Desiree. "I know you don't want to die," he said, feeling sexually excited from both the weapon and power he held over the woman. "Take off your clothes."

"What do you want with that imitation of a woman?" Madeleine demanded in desperate jealousy.

Matamore motioned at Madeleine. "I told you to leave the room. Do as I say!"

Desiree backed away but bumped into the bed. She could read the look of determination and purpose in Matamore's expression despite his dark glasses.

"I said for you to strip naked," Matamore said. "I want to see your breasts—the pink nipples—" He edged closer to Desiree.

"Philippe!" The anguish in Madeleine's voice was like the cry of a dying dove.

Desiree slowly reached up and carefully buttoned her collar, pointedly closing her body from view. She stared into his face insolently. She dropped her hand. "You go to hell!"

Matamore started to snarl, but his mouth opened wide. An expression of surprise and pain came over his face, and he slowly turned to stagger away from Desiree, the machete buried deep in his back.

Madeleine, tears streaming down her face, spoke in a broken, sobbing voice. "*Pourquoi, Philippe? Comment je t'aime!* You made me kill you!"

Philippe Matamore's only gesture at infidelity proved to be his last. He hit the floor, and blood cascaded heavily out of the massive wound.

Madeleine turned toward Desiree who was now kneeling beside the bed, reaching under it for the Uzi. The Haitian woman's face was a mask of uncontrolled hatred. "White devil bitch! What have you done to my man?" She took one step, then stopped.

Desiree raised the barrel of the submachine gun. "I've no desire to work up more sweat, dear. It's so unladylike.'' Since noise would spoil the surprise necessary for Track and Company's exfiltration, Desiree really didn't want to fire the Uzi.

Madeleine continued forward until she loomed over the smaller woman. She started to lunge, but Desiree's hand, shaped into a *nakayubi ipponken* knuckle fist, punched into her throat. The lovely black woman grabbed at her neck, trying to suck air through the mangled tissue. She staggered back, then collapsed from lack of oxygen.

The end was mercifully quick.

Desiree spun on her knee at the new sound in the room. Dan Track, Zulu and George stood there. Track walked over to her and helped her to her feet. ''Looks like you've accomplished this mission quite handily, my dear.''

''There's only one thing left,'' Desiree said, getting to her feet. ''And that's to get away and rejoin our good friend Kiowa O'Keefe.''

''That looks like the easy part now,'' Track said. ''Let's go.''

He turned toward the door and stopped.

Old Arlo's nephew and three other men stood there with FN FAL 7.62 mm rifles leveled dead at them.

Hemmed in tight, Track and Company had no place to go.

20

Track desperately scanned the room for something—anything—that would give him an opportunity to break the bind he and the others were in.

"Don't make a move," Harry said. He read the desperation in Track's stance. "Any sudden action will be your last."

The men with the Jamaican, instantly recognized by Track, Zulu and George as those who were with him in the brawl at the waterfront saloon, quickly and expertly fanned out in the room. Their weapons were arranged for an instant crossfire that would cut down Track and Company in the blink of an eye.

"Just stand steady, Major Track," Harry continued. "You'll shortly see there's no reason for alarm on your part."

Track was confused. "I beg your pardon?" He looked closer to make sure that, indeed, this was Harry. But there was something decidedly different about him. His manner of speech and demeanor were not those that had been evident when he'd been in his Uncle Arlo's shack or, most assuredly, in the Blue Lantern Saloon on the night of the brawl.

"Before anything rash occurs, Major, please let me assure you that you are in no danger. I am Sergeant Harry Miller of Jamaican police intelligence," Harry said. "These men with me are part of the same division."

George Beegh's eyes opened wide. "Holy shit! They're the fuzz!"

"Exactly," Harry Miller said. "You must trust me on that point, however. I most certainly do not carry proper identification while undercover."

Track laughed. "Are you here to bust us over that fight in the Blue Lantern?"

Sergeant Harry Miller smiled. "Not at all, Major. We're on your side, really. Let's everyone relax now, shall we? It would be tragic if something stupid happened." He motioned to his men, and all slung their assault rifles over their shoulders. Harry walked across the room with an outstretched right hand. "I'm also your contact for The Consortium. We've had you under surveillance since you arrived in Kingston. We brawled with you in the Blue Lantern that most memorable of evenings to keep you from proceeding further in the Robbers' Roost neighborhood. We preferred that you go to sea to carry on the mission. As a matter of fact, we're here to link up with you for your exfiltration."

Track shook hands, then sat down on the bed. "Pardon me—Harry—but this is a hell of a lot to take all of a sudden."

"It certainly is," Zulu said.

Desiree was puzzled. She nudged Track. "Where do you know these policemen from?"

Track laughed. "Actually, we got in a fight with them in a bar."

"And they didn't arrest you?" Desiree asked.

Harry smiled in amusement. "There's a bit of story to that, Miss Goth."

"You know my name?"

"Of course. Our pilot Kiowa O'Keefe has undoubtedly briefed Sir Abner on the situation, so he now knows the truth, as well," Harry said. "We, like the American police, find ourselves somewhat limited in our effectiveness at times by legal procedures."

Track nodded knowingly. "And working with The Consortium helps you to get around certain restrictions, right?"

"Yes," Harry said. "But we're strictly on our own—like at this moment."

"But what about Old Arlo?" Zulu asked. "Is he really your uncle?"

"He most certainly is," Harry answered. "We're quite close, actually. The happiest memories of my boyhood are of those days I spent sailing with Uncle Arlo."

"He knows you're a policeman, then?" Zulu asked.

"Of course. As a matter of fact, it was he who alerted me about people disappearing from their boats," Harry explained. "He is a real sailor, and some old acquaintances of his at the Queen Anne Yacht Club had sought his advice on numerous occasions about interesting places to sail. He's quite aged, but his mind is as alert as ever. He recalled giving directions and advice to visitors on holiday, as well. Naturally, he also remembered the names of their boats. Too many of these craft ended up on the missing-at-sea reports. He called me and I talked him into working for us."

"Where does The Consortium come in?" George asked.

"They are but one of several contacts I've developed over the five years I've been in police intelligence," Harry explained. "It's been a case of 'one hand washing the other.' I help them when I can, and they me. In this case, we are actually full partners in the benefits from wrapping things up nice and tidy."

"I can buy that," George conceded.

"You're a damned good actor, Harry," Track said.

"Thank you," Harry said. "I also have some further information for you to act on, but it is essential that we leave the island immediately. This place is a powderkeg. The populace has grown somewhat disenchanted with their former leader, and a revolution of sorts is in the making.''

Desiree pointed to Matamore's body. ''That problem has been taken care of.''

''When they find he is dead, open fighting to occupy his vacant throne will become even fiercer than it is now,'' Harry said. ''It is imperative that we go.''

''I presume you have a plan,'' Track remarked.

''Not much of one, I'm afraid,'' Harry replied. ''We are going to go en masse from here to our boat in the harbor, board her, then head out to sea to meet Sir Abner and O'Keefe.''

''Why don't we all go back to Jamaica in your boat?'' George asked.

''I'm afraid that might blow our cover,'' Harry explained. ''It is best that you return in O'Keefe's airplane.''

Zulu walked to the veranda and looked out. ''I can hear quite a lot of shouting.''

''Then it is safe to assume our departure will be a bit on the adventurous side,'' Harry Miller said. ''Shall we go?''

The Jamaican policeman led the way through the door and down the hall to the back porch. As the group descended the steps, the sounds of conflict from the village increased, and a couple of shots could be heard.

''I presume that certain factions vying for leadership have now emerged,'' Harry said. He looked at Track. ''I say, Major, would you be so kind as to walk at the front with me? That shotgun of yours looks as if it was designed for a situation like this.''

Track hurried forward to catch up with the police sergeant. ''You seem certain that there's going to be trouble.''

"Yes," Harry Miller said. "I'm afraid the various groups striving for supremacy here live by the motto of 'You're either with us or against us.' Since none of us is well-known, I presume they will consider our lot part of the opposition."

"I have several very pertinent questions to ask you," Track remarked.

"And I should be most happy to answer them for you," Harry said. "But that will have to wait until we've managed to get off this unhappy island and are back in Jamaica. Arrangements for a clandestine meeting between us have already been made."

"Fine," Track agreed. Then he changed the subject to the present situation. "I've studied a map of this island. There is a small village on the other side of this jungle grove. It stands between us and the harbor."

"We shall be fighting our way through that hamlet to the boat," Harry said.

Track was puzzled. "If we're obviously leaving the place, why would any power-hungry gang want to stop us?"

"Because they don't know who we are, or who we work for," Harry said. "The lads that take over won't want anybody leaving until they've consolidated their holdings and have everyone under their thumbs. They would not give us any benefit of doubt. As far as anyone around here is concerned, we might bring back another bunch to add to the melee."

Track nodded. "We'll have to fight our way out of here, all right."

They reached the edge of the grove and stopped. Harry pointed to a group of armed men situated at the head of the village's main street. "Here's our first encounter."

"Let's get at it," Track suggested. He tightened his grip on the SPAS-12 and moved forward with the Jamaican police sergeant.

STUBBY BOUDREAUX BENT DOWN and opened the trapdoor. He peered through the opening at the cabin cruiser tied to the floating dock below. "How y'all doin'?" he asked.

One of the men lounging in the cockpit looked up at him. "We're goddamned tired o' waitin'. That's how we're doin', pal."

"Don't worry," Stubby said. "The fellers up at the radio shack says the Coast Guard and the customs boys have moved out of the area. We can drop the load on you now."

"Hot damn! It's about time," the man said, getting to his feet. He walked to the door leading below decks on his vessel and shouted at others down there to come topside and join him.

Meanwhile, Stubby motioned to Marvin Leroy who stood nearby with a thick rope in his large hands. The line was run through a heavy-duty pulley.

"Okay, shithead. Heave!"

Marvin Leroy pulled on the rope lifting the large bale of marijuana attached to the other end. Stubby leaned against the bundle of pot and pushed it toward the trapdoor. The pulley, attached to a rail, squeaked as it rolled along the track. When the load was directly over the opening, Stubby halted his efforts.

"Y'all ready?" he shouted down.

"Lower away, Stubby."

Stubby motioned at his nephew. "Let her down easy, Marvin Leroy. I don't want you droppin' this heavy shit on their heads down there."

Marvin Leroy nodded. Then he gently let the rope ease through his huge hands. The bale slowly went through the trapdoor and down to the cockpit of the boat below.

"Okay! We got it, Stubby!" The rope was loosened and cast free. "Haul it back."

Marvin Leroy yanked on the rope until the hardware on the end of it came into view. Stubby looked back down to the boat. "There you are. I'll see you fellers on the next run."

"Right, Stubby. Thanks for the hospitality."

"Anytime," Stubby said. He lowered the door. "Let's git back out front, Marvin Leroy."

"Yes, sir, Uncle Stubby," Marvin Leroy said.

The two returned to the chandlery's front room. Stubby went outside and took his usual seat in the chair he kept there. Marvin Leroy hopped up on the dock railing.

"Another day, another dollar," Stubby said contentedly. He pulled his chewing tobacco pouch from his shirt. "This is one swell setup, Marvin Leroy."

"Yeah," his nephew said. "We're really makin' good money, huh, Uncle Stubby?"

Stubby laughed. "Even you've figgered that out, huh, boy?"

"Well, Mama tole me we was doin' right fine," Marvin Leroy said. "And when you bought that new Cadillac car I knowed things was good."

"That's right, boy."

"How's come we're makin' more money now, Uncle Stubby?" Marvin Leroy asked. "We ain't even workin' as hard as before."

"I don't know if I can explain so you'll understand, Marvin Leroy," Stubby said. "But I'll try. Okay?"

"Okay."

"There's a bunch o' folks that likes to git high off'n drugs. They use them leaves and that white powder we deal with, see? It ain't legal to have it, so they got to pay lots o' money for the stuff.''

"You don't want no police to know what we're doin', right?''

"Right,'' Stubby said. Then he put a threat in his tone. "So don't you go talkin' 'bout what we do to no strangers—got it, shithead? Even if the sumbitch ain't dressed like a cop don't mean he ain't one.''

"Yes, sir. I understand that real good,'' Marvin Leroy said.

"And that goes for women,'' Stubby elaborated. "The law uses 'em to fool you. And there's other fellers in the same business we're in that'd like to knock us out of it. We got to look for them, too. So don't you trust nobody. Okay?''

"Okay.'' Marvin Leroy thought for a few minutes. "Since folks cain't buy dope in a store, we got to sneak it to 'em. Is that it, Uncle Stubby?''

"That's it in a nutshell, boy.''

"What if the police come here?''

"We'll fight or run,'' Stubby said. "Whatever seems best at the time.''

"What if them other fellers in the same business come here, Uncle Stubby?''

"Anybody else gits kilt,'' Stubby said grimly. "Just like yore daddy or Pedro. There ain't no question about that.''

"Yes, sir, Uncle Stubby. I'll remember that real good.''

TRACK AND COMPANY, along with the four Jamaican policemen, stepped boldly out of the jungle growth and walked confidently toward the group of men standing at the head of the village's main street. Several bottles were visible among them, and it was obvious they had been drinking heavily.

One of them stepped forward with a drunken swagger. He carried a French MAT-49 submachine gun. He started to raise it.

Track snapped the SPAS-12 up to waist level and slammed off three quick shots.

The submachine gunner stumbled back under the blast as the others in the group went down like scythed rows of wheat. Another man, who had miraculously escaped being hit, sobered up quickly. He fled toward the center of the village.

Everyone—the four members of Track and Company and the four Jamaican cops—instantly aimed at him. All cut loose at once.

The fugitive simply disintegrated under the onslaught of flying slugs. In an instant he was transformed from a running man into hunks of bloody meat slammed down on the narrow street.

"Jesus!" Track said. "I'll bet that ruined his day."

The group fanned out now, sticking close to the sides of the shacks, as they moved at a slow but steady gait toward the harbor.

They suddenly received fire from their right front. While the others quickly laid down a fusillade, Track ran between a couple of shacks and circled around on the other side. The sniper was firing from a flimsy grass hut that reminded Track of *The Three Little Pigs*.

He waited until he could get a good idea where the bushwhacker was situated inside. When the man fired again, Track went into action.

The SPAS-12 roared, sending a crashing hail of buckshot through the straw. The man inside was blown through the opposite wall and dumped in an undignified heap on the street.

Track stepped out from between the other crude domiciles and started to signal an "all clear" when a movement across the narrow street caught his eye. He motioned to the others and, at the same time, aimed the SPAS-12.

"Don' shoot, *señor*!" The voice, speaking in broken English, quavered with fear.

"C'mon out," Track ordered. "And hold your hands high."

A swarthy man, obeying orders to the letter, stepped into the street. "Hey, you 'merican, man. I hear you talk. You go to a boat. I go wit' you, okay?"

Although Track knew a prisoner would be of particular value to Sergeant Harry Miller, he was hesitant. "Why should we give you a ride?"

"I got *dinero*—money, man. I was the radio operator up at the mansion," he pleaded. "I ain't in nobody's gang, man. I just wanna get outta here!"

"We'll take you, then," Track said, winking at Harry. "If you promise to answer a couple of questions."

"Sure, man. *¿Cómo no?*"

"Well, then," Track said. He motioned to the others. "Shall we continue?"

"An excellent suggestion," Zulu said.

A roaring battle had developed off at the opposite side of the hamlet by then. The main showdown between the pirate factions had broken out. Track and Company, along with their Jamaican friends, had a clear run to the harbor.

Then another problem presented itself.

Since there was no dock, they had to get a launch to take them out to the boat the Jamaicans had used to come to the island. A quick look up and down the little beach showed there were several of the small craft a hundred yards away—in the direction of the main battle that now was escalating in intensity.

There are times when logical, step-by-step planning and evaluation of a situation is not only impossible but downright dangerous because of the time it takes.

This was one of those moments.

The group of nine people, following Track's lead, ran toward the launches. The frightened radio operator stumbled along in their midst. A few seconds before they reached the boats, Track yelled his orders. "George! Zulu! You're the drivers. Rev those babies up fast! The rest of you make a perimeter and start shooting!"

His instructions were followed to the letter. Six weapons—one Franchi SPAS-12 shotgun, one Uzi submachine gun, and four FN FAL rifles—lay out a curtain of covering fire that blew down three nearby shacks.

A half dozen of the pirates had spotted the group's run to the launches rushed down from another street leading to the anchorage, bent on intercepting them.

All six firearms swung toward the buccaneers, kicking out a rain of death.

The pirates, caught square in the center of the fusillade, sprawled grotesquely under the salvos as the steel wind flung them to the ground.

The launches' outboard motors were roaring, and the gunners jumped aboard. Track grabbed the radio operator by the collar and hauled him bodily into a boat. George and Zulu displayed the nautical skills they had developed over the previous several weeks by backing out rapidly into the lagoon, then turning around and heading for the boats.

Sergeant Harry Miller pointed. "The large white Cheoy Lee. See it dead ahead?"

"Right you are," Zulu said.

Looking toward shore, Track could see that the fighting on the island was moving up from the village to the old French plantation mansion.

"Wait'll they find that Philippe Matamore is dead," Track said.

The radio operator's eyes opened wide. "Matamore is dead?" he asked.

"As that proverbial doornail," Track answered.

The Hispanic crossed himself. "*¡Gracias a Dios y todos los santos!* I'm glad to get outta there. That crazy Haitian liked to shoot the peoples he don' like in the head wit' his *pistola automatica*. Sometimes he push it in *sus caras*— their faces, man!"

"Sounds to me like Matamore's death will cut the bloodshed on the Spanish Main by one hell of a lot," Track said.

"But that'll only be half the battle won as far as I'm concerned," Harry Miller said. "We've got to destroy the contact men for this operation."

Track looked at the prisoner. "If you're really grateful to us for hauling you outta here, you'll show your appreciation by letting us in on a few facts."

"Sure, *señor*! But I will tell you nothing until we are gone from Ile-a-Salut," the man said. "You kill me, and you know *nada*—nothing!"

Harry Miller snarled at him. "How do we know your information will really interest us?"

The radioman smiled uneasily. "I t'ink you are the law, no? And you want the name of the Matamore's contact man in Jamaica."

Track smiled without humor. "You know what will happen if we find you're lying to us?"

The prisoner nodded. "*Sí, señor*. I know."

Both launches bumped against the vessel at that point. Track, in the bow of the first boat, climbed aboard, then reached down and gave Harry a hand. "What are you going to do about the contact man in Jamaica?"

"Even after that radio operator gives us his name, we will still have to get him to talk," Harry said, climbing over the railing.

"Would it save the Jamaican taxpayers a lot of money if you left that to us?" Track asked.

Harry smiled and nodded. "We would certainly appreciate your efforts."

"Let's firm that up," Track said, using one of his favorite expressions.

George and Zulu grabbed their prisoner and hustled him below to isolate him from the group.

Track looked around at the cabin cruiser. "This is a beauty. Is it a police vessel?"

"No," Harry explained as the others came aboard. "We actually borrowed her from a member of The Consortium."

"I presume he has it insured," Track said.

"Undoubtedly, Major," Harry said, appreciating the humor. Two of the Jamaican policemen went to the control console and started the engines. Within moments the boat was moving out to the open sea.

"While we are on our way to drop you off at O'Keefe's airplane, I shall brief you," Harry said. "You'll arrive in Kingston long before us. By the time we get there, we will have the name of the contact man from our friend below. We will be able to direct you to the next link in the pirate chain."

"Are you sure there's a next one?"

"Very much so," Harry Miller answered. "Of course you will have to get that name from the contact man."

"You're hinting that we should do all the interrogating, right?" Track asked.

"Right," Harry Miller answered.

"Are we limited in our methods?" Track asked.

"You are not policemen, are you?" Harry asked. "There are no specific rules that restrict your conduct."

"I understand," Track said flatly.

"And when you know who that individual is, he will have to be dealt with and terminated quickly and efficiently."

Track nodded. "I suppose The Consortium wants us to do that particular job, too, huh?"

"Yes," Harry answered. "And so do the United States Coast Guard and Customs Service."

21

Track drove the rented Toyota sedan into the visitors' section of the parking lot.

He swung the automobile into the nearest space, then killed the engine. He glanced over at Sir Abner who sat beside him. "This is going to be particularly unpleasant for you."

Sir Abner nodded. "Yes. I'm afraid so. But things will be sorted out, I'm sure."

George Beegh and Zulu, both in the back seat, sat silently.

Sir Abner turned and glared at them. "Well, damn it! Don't either of you have anything to say?"

Zulu shrugged his massive shoulders. "It is unfortunate. What more can one say."

"Not exactly," Track corrected him. "That radio operator from Ile-a-Salut sang loud and long about the guy. He was burning his candle at both ends."

"He's no phony," George said. "The guy was exactly what he said he was."

"I suppose that makes me responsible," Sir Abner said. He opened the door and got out of the car. "If you are in the least bit interested, let me tell you that I am not harboring the slightest feelings of guilt."

The other three men joined him beside the Toyota. Track felt sympathy for the older man. "Jesus Christ, Sir Abner!" he exclaimed. "It's ridiculous for you to feel at fault, anyway. You're letting the British class system get the better of you."

"It's a damned fine system!" Sir Abner snapped. "Now which bungalow are we searching for?" He looked toward the numerous rented houses scattered around the walks that led from the parking lot.

"Thirty B," Track said. "It's supposed to be on the far end. Toward the sea."

"Ah, yes," Sir Abner said. "It would be close to the ocean, wouldn't it?"

The Briton led the others down the walk. They went through the little housing development to the last domicile that sat on a small rise on the well-cared-for grounds. There was an excellent view of the Caribbean, stretching out to the southern horizon.

It was quite early in the evening, and the blue-greenness of the sea was particularly startling.

The four men stepped up to the front door of Bungalow 30 B. Sir Abner knocked lightly. He waited a couple of moments, then rapped again.

The door opened and Bernard Durham-Jones, Lieutenant-Commander, Royal Navy, Retired, and Commodore of the Queen Anne Yacht Club of Kingston, Jamaica, appeared. He wore a dark blazer bearing the coat of arms of his former service, a white scarf around his neck, charcoal gray slacks and expensive Italian shoes.

"Hello!" he said, happily surprised. "Upon my word, it is Mr. Hunter and my friend Chesterton. I was just about to go out." He characteristically ignored the presence of Zulu and George, whom he considered little more than servants.

Sir Abner cleared his throat nervously. "I am Sir Abner, actually—that is, Lord Chesterton, if you please."

Durham-Jones's face paled a bit. "I say!" But he regained his composure. "Do come in, my friends."

Zulu, a serious expression on his face, said, "George and I shall wait out here."

Track and Sir Abner stepped inside, and Durham-Jones shut the door. "You say you are Lord Chesterton."

"I actually prefer to be addressed as Sir Abner," the other Englishman said. "I earned that. The title was simply an accident of birth."

"As you wish—Sir Abner," Durham-Jones responded. "I must admit to feeling a bit confused and befuddled at the moment over all this. But at any rate, what might I do for you?"

"This is quite awkward, Durham-Jones," Sir Abner said, "and the best way to handle it is straight out."

"Of course."

Track remained silent, the Beretta 9 mm nestled snugly in the shoulder holster under his tropical suit coat.

"Some rather serious charges have been leveled against you, old man," Sir Abner said. "And most unfortunately, they've been substantiated."

"Charges? Against me?" Durham-Jones laughed. "What sort of bloody ridiculous charges?"

"I'm afraid," Sir Abner said, "that you've been positively linked with a band of drug-smuggling murderers."

"I say! Poppycock that, what?"

Track was growing weary of the tedious way the interrogation was going. "The radio operator from the Ile-a-Salut in Haiti has spilled his guts. You're up to your fucking ears in trouble."

"My God, man!" Sir Abner shouted. "Make a clean breast of it. You're an English gentleman."

Durham-Jones was silent for a few moments. When he spoke, he did so in a low but distinct voice. "And a heroin addict."

"Good Lord!" Sir Abner exclaimed.

"It came from a war wound actually," Durham-Jones said. "Never healed properly. I've been in constant pain of one sort or another since 1945. In fact, it cut my career short, thus I am a retired lieutenant-commander rather than a captain or admiral."

Sir Abner's eyes were stone cold. "That is absolutely no excuse, Durham-Jones."

"And I'm not using it as one," the retired Royal Navy man said. "I'm simply explaining things, so I don't appear the total blackguard."

"But surely you could have used narcotics without falling in with a gang of bloody murderers," Sir Abner said.

"Illicit drug use is an expensive pastime, old boy," Durham-Jones explained. "I'm afraid I embezzled some funds from the yacht club on various occasions. When the accountant came across it, he coerced me. He was a money man for the smugglers, and he threatened me with exposure if I didn't cooperate in getting boats for his organization."

"Disgraceful!" Sir Abner said.

"Good Lord, Sir Abner! I didn't know they were murdering those poor people until...until..." He momentarily lost control, his eyes misting. He struggled to regain his composure. "Being a commodore, even of a yacht club, meant everything to me, old boy. It was my life after the unfortunate end of my career. I was more than just a bloody retired officer living in genteel poverty. I was somebody—and the smugglers paid me for the information, too. I was able to have a respectable life-style, and even a small boat of my own."

Track decided not to waste any more time. "We understand you have a contact in Florida. We want his name."

"Of course. I shan't say it aloud." He smiled weakly at Sir Abner. "Those of us educated in England's grand old public schools were taught to never snitch—right, Sir Abner?''

"Quite right."

"I shall write the name on a piece of paper," Durham-Jones said. "That should suffice."

He walked over the desk drawer and opened it. He stepped back immediately when Track drew the Beretta. "Word of a gentleman. I shan't pull a weapon from here."

Sir Abner looked over at Track. "Let him do it."

Durham-Jones took a scrap of paper and a pen. He scribbled on it, then folded it and laid it down on the desk. "There you are."

"Thank you," Sir Abner said. He stepped toward the desk and stopped.

Durham-Jones had pulled a Webley revolver from the desk drawer. It was pointed directly at Sir Abner, but he spoke to Track. "If you should shoot me, I would pull the trigger by reflex. I fear that would be the end of Sir Abner."

Track, frowning, slowly lowered the Beretta.

Sir Abner was aghast. "I thought you were a gentleman."

"I am," Durham-Jones said. "And I am about to do the gentlemanly thing."

He backed toward the door leading to the bedroom. "Goodbye, chaps."

Durham-Jones rushed inside the other room. Immediately a shot exploded in the bungalow.

Zulu and George, both armed, rushed into the small house.

Sir Abner stepped into the bedroom. He looked down at the suicide, and nodded his head in approval. "He did the right thing."

Track, more pragmatic and less impressed, went to the desk and unfolded the paper Durham-Jones had left there. A name was written on it: Stubby Boudreaux.

22

Pablo Ortiz was wide awake despite the early hour. He'd just done a couple of lines of coke and was feeling alert, important and ready to take on the world. Even the dawn seemed remarkable to him as he walked his security post on Stubby Boudreaux's marina.

A boat whistle, sounding melodic and sonorous to his dope-fudged ears, blasted just inside the breakwater. Pablo looked out in that direction to see a beautiful white Cheoy Lee cabin cruiser approaching, its bow plowing a smooth, foamy furrow in the water.

Ten minutes later the boat made a lazy circle. Then, with engines reversed, it backed smoothly into the slip where Pablo stood.

A young man tossed him a line. "Tie her up, will ya, pal?"

"Sure!" Pablo said cheerfully. He'd done that task many times as a boy in La Habana. He flipped the line over the dock post rather clumsily—though in his befuddled mind he saw the action as rapid and smooth.

The man on the boat jumped off the stern and secured the big boat on that end. He waved again to Pablo. "Hey, pal. Pretty early in the day, isn't it?"

"You bet," Pablo said. He surveyed the boat as carefully as he could, noting it would make a hell of a dope runner. When things finally got back to normal down south, he'd point this one out to the boys on Ile-a-Salut.

They'd make short work of the people aboard, and the gang would have another fine vessel to use in their operations.

"You want a cup of coffee or something?" the man said. "I just put on a fresh pot."

Pablo shook his head, then considered what might happen if Stubby Boudreaux came out and caught him on this cocaine high. He figured he'd better take some of the edge off it. "Have you got any liquor, man? I could use a shot of *escocés*—Scotch."

"Sure, pal. C'mon aboard."

Pablo stepped up on the gunwale and dropped into the cockpit. "Would you make that a double, man?"

George Beegh pulled the .45 Colt Commander from his waist and shoved it into Pablo's face. He smiled. "I sure as hell will make that a double shot unless you do what I say."

Pablo was ushered down below where Dan Track, Zulu, Desiree and Sir Abner waited. The befuddled doper caught a brief glimpse of Track's stiletto just before it slipped through the flesh of his throat.

Pablo gasped, striking out, but the massive injection of morphine, deftly administered by Desiree, almost immediately stilled his struggling and pain.

Desiree tossed the hypodermic aside as Track wiped the knife on his trousers. He looked down at the now dead man. "It's assholes like you that make it a dog-eat-dog world. Now you've had yours, Fido."

Then Track and Company, fully armed, moved out to the job at hand.

Desiree quickly went up to the entrance to the marina and took cover behind a pile of rotting fishing nets. Her job would be to keep the enemy hemmed in—or potential infiltrators locked out—using her Uzi submachine gun as a persuader.

Sir Abner and Zulu took off in the opposite direction, hurrying to a small wooden shack out toward the breakwater. When they reached it, they squatted and checked their watches.

Dan Track and George Beegh walked slowly and quietly down the dock to position themselves at the door of Stubby's chandlery.

Then they waited.

Sir Abner scrutinized his watch as the second hand swept up to twelve. Five seconds before it got there he raised a finger. The second before it reached that point, he dropped the digit. Zulu, the concussion grenade ready, pulled the pin. He let the safety spoon pop, then quickly opened the door of the little shack and tossed the device inside.

The resulting explosion caused the boards of the crude building to strain outward against the nails holding them in place. Zulu pulled the damaged door free from its hinges and charged in with Sir Abner directly behind him.

Nine-millimeter slugs from the Englishman's Sterling and the black man's Uzi sprayed out. The two men manning the radio-radar equipment caught the brunt of the volleys and were flung bodily into the sophisticated equipment. They had been so stunned by the grenade that they hardly realized what was happening.

At the exact moment the grenade detonated, Track and George kicked in the door of the chandlery and charged inside. A guard, who had been half dozing on the counter, rolled off, snarling at the intruders.

The revolver in his hand was blown back into his body by the force of the blast from Track's SPAS-12. George skipped past the man as he bounced off the counter, rushing through the door behind it.

Another gunsel, comfortably asleep on the cot there, sat up in time to catch three quick shots from George's AR-15

9 mm. He was slammed back to the pillow, his blood soaking it and the mattress from the trio of fatal wounds.

Outside, between the chandlery and machine shop, another thug emerged. It appeared to him like a full-blown gang war had just broken out. In the event of raids by any of the competition, it was his job to notify the big boss in Miami. He wasted no time and hurried for the pay phone on the street.

Desiree leaped out from behind the fishing nets, leveled the Uzi on the guy and swept him away with one quick burst. He staggered off the side of the dock in a comical little death dance, splashing into the dirty water.

Desiree ducked back behind cover, waiting for any more folks with ideas about passing her.

Sir Abner and Zulu ran off the stone breakwater and back onto the dock. Their next objective was a small boathouse between themselves and the chandlery.

They blasted through the door of the building and rushed inside. There were three sleek motorboats moored in the interior. Wordlessly and rapidly, the duo dropped two incendiary grenades in each one. These AM-M14's, the same used to send the *Fancy Free* to her glorious end, hissed loudly in the confines of the structure.

On the way out, Zulu had an idea. He stopped long enough to hurl his last grenade, an Mk1 illuminating model, into some fuel drums situated in one corner.

"I suggest we move quickly," he said.

"Of course," Sir Abner said.

They had taken no more than a dozen steps when the place went up with a swoosh of ignited gasoline.

The concussion from the blast knocked them both violently to the dock, rolling them over until Sir Abner almost fell into the water. He hung on to the edge of the dock until Zulu got to his feet and ran over to haul him back up.

The unplanned destruction of the boathouse caused Track and George to run out of the chandlery's storage area to see what was going on.

"Check that out, George," Track ordered. "I'll clear the chandlery and meet you outside."

"Right." George hurried off to where Zulu and Sir Abner were situated.

Track went back inside Stubby's store. The messy cadaver of the first guard was spread all over the counter. The dead man on the cot had soaked it full with his blood. Track went to the door he'd started to investigate when the boathouse blew up.

Holding the SPAS-12 ready, he kicked open the door and fired a solid shot, then a blast of buckshot before stepping into the room. He saw it was someone's rather austere living quarters.

A rotund, familiar figure was huddled in the corner. "Who the hell are you?"

Track recognized Stubby Boudreaux. "Stand up real slow, fat man."

Stubby raised his hands and complied. He stood waiting for whatever the stranger wanted. When Track stepped farther into the room, the Cajun squinted his eyes until he finally saw who it was in the dim light.

"Ain't you off the *Fancy Free*?"

Track nodded. "That's me."

"Goddamn that boat," Stubby said angrily. "Ever since you showed up here, I've had nothin' but trouble."

"Your troubles are just starting," Track said.

Stubby smiled. "I could say the same for you." Then he grimaced and yelled, "Git him, shithead!"

The blow came out of the shadows and Track was knocked across ten feet of space to slam into the wall. The SPAS-12 fell from his hands as he hit the floor.

"You better leave my Uncle Stubby alone!"

Track, dazed, looked up to see the gigantic form of Marvin Leroy Firpo looming above him. The kid was clearly pissed off, his hammy fists doubled for action.

"Goddamn it!" Stubby bellowed. "Don't just stand there, you dumb shithead, you! Kick hell outta the bastard!"

Track rolled quickly away, the motion easing him away from most of the big shoe's contact with his body.

The swings that made contact hurt like hell.

Leaping to his feet, Track found himself immediately overwhelmed by Marvin Leroy. The kid grabbed him by the front of his shirt and picked him up, throwing him hard against the wall. Track's head was cracked hard, and he fell forward to catch a wild uppercut that hit him dead center on the forehead.

Track instinctively performed a desperate *ushiro geri* kick from the side. He had the satisfaction of feeling it hit solid into Marvin Leroy's midsection.

"Ooof!" Marvin Leroy complained about a kick that would have disabled anyone else. "That *hurt*!"

"Try this," Track suggested. He shot several old-fashioned right and left jabs in rapid succession, his knuckles scraping raw on Marvin Leroy's unshaven chin.

The only effect this had on the kid was to make his head snap back and forth. But he took enough offense from the attack to slam a huge paw down directly on the top of Track's head.

Track felt as if his skull had been driven down to his asshole. With neck vertebrae screaming, he staggered backward, defending against some more clumsy, but extremely heavy, overhand blows by performing alternating *jodan uke* forearm blocks.

Stubby cackled in hysterical glee. "Take 'at, you sumbitch! Ol' Marvin Leroy's gonna be all over yore ass like the plague! He's gonna fuck you up worser than polio!

When he gits done with you, people ain't gonna ask where you *been*, they're gonna ask how you got *loose*!''

With Marvin Leroy's heavy hands and fists raining down on him like lobbed-in mortar shells, Track was inclined to agree with Stubby's prediction.

Finally, Track dived inside the clumsy attack and drove both hands straight up. They bashed into Marvin Leroy's chin so hard that even that heavy guy was raised a couple of inches off the floor.

"Ouch!"

Track then slammed out two lightning-fast *seiken chudan tsuki* straight punches.

"Ow! Ow!" Marvin Leroy, truly angry now, picked Track up and threw him toward the opposite wall.

Track hit the wall back-first and head-down, collapsing to the floor in time to have Marvin Leroy grab him by the feet.

"I'm gonna bust yore head!" Marvin Leroy yelled. He whirled Track around three times before hurling him back against the same wall.

Track, his arms up to protect his head, collided hard. Dizzy and disoriented, he made contact with the floor facedown.

Marvin Leroy again picked him up, this time under the arms. He shook Track hard, pressing his face against Track's. "How come yo're such a bad feller?" He lifted Track up so high that he repeatedly bounced Track's head against the ceiling. "What would yore mama think o' you?"

Track's neck, already sore as hell, felt as if a red-hot clamp had been tightened down on it. His head, making monotonously regular contact with each upward motion of Marvin Leroy's powerful arms, was also a mass of pain.

Track hunched his shoulder muscles as he gathered his energy, then exploded into one of the hardest *hiji jodan ate* elbow smashes he had ever done in his life.

Marvin Leroy's eyes took on a blank stare and he dropped the man.

Track hit him again with the opposite elbow, this time performing a faultless *hiji chudan ate*.

Marvin Leroy backpedaled, then stood swaying a bit, trying to fight the daze that washed over him.

Track bellowed and flew into a *yoko tobi geri* flying kick that contacted square with Marvin Leroy's face.

The boy went down like a 250-pound bag of wet sand.

Stubby screamed in rage. "Git up, you shithead, you! Git up and finish kickin' his goddamned ass!"

Track, now stunned beyond comprehension after making that final superhuman effort, lost his balance and his knees gave way. He fell to the floor.

Stubby ran over and tried to pull Marvin Leroy to his feet. "Git up! Git up! Git up!" He glared in furious hatred at Track. "What'd you do to this boy, you no-good sumbitch!"

Track, his head cleared a trifle, raised his eyes and glowered at the Cajun. Snarling, Track fought dizziness and disorientation to get to his feet and lunge toward Stubby.

Stubby, now so angry that he couldn't speak, leaped back out of reach. Then he spotted the SPAS-12 assault shotgun lying on the floor. Sputtering and spitting in a fury, he raced over to the weapon and picked it up. He swung the bore toward Track and slipped his finger inside the trigger guard.

The 9 mm bullet from George Beegh's AR-15 went in just below Stubby's right eye. It exited out his left ear, taking most of his face with it and flinging it across the room.

The SPAS-12 was pointing straight up when it went off.

George walked over to the dead Cajun and retrieved the shotgun. Then, helping Track to his feet, he half carried him through the chandlery to the dock outside.

Sir Abner, Zulu and Desiree appeared at the front door almost simultaneously. Sir Abner checked his watch. "It is imperative that we exfiltrate immediately."

The whole place was on fire. There was only a narrow path clear on the dock that led to their boat. The flames threatened to claim that, too.

Desiree rushed to Track, slipping her arm around him. *"Chéri!"* she cried.

"This place is going up fast!" George yelled. "Let's get a move on!"

Track, now able to talk, walked unsteadily between her and George. "I'll be okay in a minute, but, damn! My neck is killing me!"

Within moments they were back aboard the Cheoy Lee. Sir Abner started up the engines while George and Zulu cast her free from the dock. When they jumped aboard, the Englishman pressed forward on the throttles and the big vessel roared out of the slip, heading for the open sea.

THE SKIPPER of the Coast Guard cutter kept his binoculars trained on the white boat until it became a white blur on the horizon.

"Well?"

"I think I hear a disturbance, sir," the CPO said with a grin. "Maybe we should investigate."

"You're right, chief," the skipper said. "It sounds like it came from Stubby Boudreaux's marina, doesn't it?"

"I would say so, sir."

The officer raised his binoculars again. "Let's wait a bit," he said. When the whiteness of the Cheoy Lee had disappeared over the horizon, he took the glasses away from his eyes. "Okay, chief. Let's go now."

The cutter moved slowly through the water, turning landward toward the burning mess that was once a marina.

23

Desiree Goth was gone.

A few quick questions to the Queen Anne Yacht Club's manager had confirmed she'd checked out of her bungalow at a little past midnight on the same night they had returned from hitting the marina. When the taxi driver who had picked her up was finally located, he reported taking the beautiful young woman to an apartment house in the suburbs.

Even Sergeant Harry Miller got nowhere in the attempt to track her farther.

Desiree Goth was truly gone.

Zulu surmised it was a former contact from her gunrunning days. "No sense in looking for her," he announced sadly. "If she has disappeared, so have the people with whom she linked up."

Stunned and shocked, Track had spent the next morning angrily knocking down double shots of Seagram's Seven. Sir Abner joined him at the yacht club's bar.

He ordered a gin and tonic, then looked into his younger friend's face. "I'm not surprised she left, old boy."

"Did she say anything to you about where she was heading?"

"No, nothing like that," Sir Abner said, taking his drink from the bartender. "She was in a turmoil, y'know. In love with you, yet an independent person, able to take care of herself and direct her own destiny. Except, that is, for the emotional befuddlement she endured over you."

"Zulu's not taking this too good, either," Track said. "He was her partner for years. Now he feels he's been left in the lurch for something he's unknowingly done to offend her."

"He'll have to live with it—like you," Sir Abner said. "But you both may rest assured we shall all see Desiree Goth when she's ready. She most certainly is not out of our lives by any stretch of the imagination."

Track stared into his drink. "My beautiful, mysterious dream woman."

"You love her dearly, don't you, old boy?" Sir Abner asked.

Instead of answering, Track finished his drink. "Let's see about getting a plane back to the States, huh?"

EPILOGUE

The dining room in Track's New Mexico ranch house was the scene of a special celebration complete with cake and champagne.

George Beegh's article on the 9 mm AR-15 rifle had been bought by *Firearms World* magazine. Not only had he received a rather healthy check, but the managing editor had requested he do another article for them. This time they wanted an extensive field test performed and written up on the Beretta automatic that the U.S. Armed Forces were adopting for use.

Tassels LaTour cut the cake she'd baked for the occasion. The ex-burlesque queen who kept her sixty-three-year-old body as shapely as ever through a strict regimen of diet and exercise, was Track's housekeeper. She and the cat, Dorothy, cared for the premises during the owner's absences. She passed a plate to Track. "What do you think of your nephew's literary efforts?"

"I'm pleasantly surprised," Track said. "I didn't even know he'd submitted anything."

"I didn't want you to know in case I got a rejection slip," George said. "I sent it in just before we joined you out in California."

Sir Abner laughed. "We all knew about it. But George had sworn us to silence."

"I had an expert check it out for me," George said. "When Desiree showed up here—"

A mood of gloom settled over the festivities at the mention of the missing woman's name.

"Well, she read it and said it was complete and organized right."

Tassels wanted to lighten up the mood. She nudged Zulu. "I actually made two cakes when I heard you were coming here."

Zulu smiled. "Well, Miss LaTour, you are an excellent cook. I guarantee you that whatever you have prepared, I shall consume most lustily."

Tassels laughed. "Damn! Don't you just love the way he talks?" She pointed at Sir Abner. "Him too."

Track went to the champagne bucket and took out the bottle. He walked around the table filling everyone's glasses. He returned to his chair and raised his own.

"To George's article."

Everyone responded to the toast.

Zulu added, "And to his future writing career."

Again the glasses were raised.

The phone rang and Tassels scurried away to answer it. Zulu took a bite of cake. "Mmm! I am most certainly glad that Miss LaTour made two of these."

Tassels returned. "It's for you, Sir Abner."

"Oh, drat!" The English gentleman got up. "Please excuse me." He hurried to the other room.

"By the way, did you see in the newspaper about Stubby's marina?" George asked.

"I haven't read anything since we returned," Track said.

"It seems the place was completely destroyed," George said with a wink. "Set back the doper operation quite a bit. The law figures it was a rival gang that hit them."

"Too bad we didn't get a chance to nab the real Mr. Big," Track said. "We'd have found out who he was if Stubby was still alive."

"Indeed," Zulu agreed. "But I think George's response to his conduct with your shotgun was the correct one."

"I agree!" Track said. "Most heartily."

"They mentioned one survivor," George said. "Ol' Marvin Leroy was found staggering out of the burning marina. A court declared him mentally incompetent and the state of Florida is now caring for him. They put him in some training program for the retarded."

"His problems ended with Stubby's death," Zulu remarked.

Everyone turned to look when Sir Abner returned to the room. "I say! The Consortium has another task for you."

"What is it this time?" Track asked. "A horde of Mongol invaders sweeping across Europe?"

"Oh, nothing quite that exciting, old boy," Sir Abner said. "This involves an insured calendar."

"A calendar!" George exclaimed. "What the hell is so special about a calendar that somebody would buy an insurance policy on it?"

"This one is quite an antique, old boy," Sir Abner said. "Its origins have been traced to the ancient Incan empire of Peru. The calendar in question is made of solid gold and studded with precious gems."

"Must be priceless!" Zulu said.

"I should say so," Sir Abner replied.

Track didn't look so much on the bright side. "It sounds like something someone would kill for."

"Most certainly," Sir Abner said. Then he turned to Tassels. "I say, Miss LaTour. May I have another piece of the absolutely marvelous cake?"

ERIC HELM

VIETNAM: GROUND ZERO

An elite jungle fighting group of strike-and-hide specialists fight a dirty war half a world away from home. This is more than action adventure. Every novel in this series is a piece of Vietnam history brought to life, from the Battle for Hill 875 to the Tet Offensive and the terror of the infamous Hanoi Hilton POW camp, told through the eyes of an American Special Forces squad. These books cut close to the bone, telling it the way it really was.

"Vietnam at Ground Zero is where this book is written. The author has been there, and he knows. I salute him and I recommend this book to my friends."

—Don Pendleton,
creator of The Executioner

Watch for VIETNAM: GROUND ZERO beginning in August from Gold Eagle Books, #1 publisher of adventures.

VGZ-

MORE ACTION!
MORE SUSPENSE!
NEW LOOK!

THE EXECUTIONER

MACK BOLAN

Beginning in July, watch out for America's number-one hero, Mack Bolan, in more spectacular, more gut-wrenching missions.

The Executioner continues to live large in bigger, bolder stories that can only be told in 256 pages.

Get into the heart of the man and the heart of the action with the first big entry, **The Trial**.

In this gripping adventure, Bolan is captured and placed on trial for his life—accused by the government he had sworn to serve. And the prosecution is hunting for the soldier's head.

Gold Eagle Books is giving readers what they asked for. You've never read action-adventure like this before!

Nile Barrabas and the Soldiers of Barrabas are the

SOBs

by Jack Hild

Nile Barrabas is a nervy son of a bitch who was the last American soldier out of Vietnam and the first man into a new kind of action. His warriors, called the Soldiers of Barrabas, have one very simple ambition: to do what the Marines can't or won't do. Join the Barrabas blitz! Each book hits new heights—this is brawling at its best!

"Nile Barrabas is one tough SOB himself. . . . A wealth of detail. . . . SOBs does the job!"
—*West Coast Review of Books*

GOLD EAGLE

Available wherever paperbacks are sold.

SOBs-1

4 FREE BOOKS
1 FREE GIFT
NO RISK
NO OBLIGATION
NO KIDDING